With thanks to the Tiwi Land Council, the Indigenous Literacy Foundation, Marnie O'Bryan, Alison Lester, Tictac Moore, Austin Wonaeamirri Jr, Jilamara Arts and Crafts Association, Hannah Raisin, Will Heathcote, Clair Hume and Craig Bate for their help in making this book.

I would like to thank all the people who looked after me in Paris as well as the Australian Embassy, especially Josh Young, and the Ancestors who look after everyone and kept me strong when I was lost.
—Glen Farmer Illortaminni

First published in Australia in 2025 by Thames & Hudson Australia
Wurundjeri Country, 132A Gwynne Street, Cremorne, Victoria 3121

First published in the United States of America in 2025
By Thames & Hudson Inc.
500 Fifth Avenue
New York, New York 10110

28 27 26 5 4 3

ISBN 978-1-760-76494-4
ISBN 978-1-760-76534-7 (U.S. edition)

NATIONAL LIBRARY OF AUSTRALIA
A catalogue record for this book is available from the National Library of Australia

Designed by Ashlea O'Neill | Salt Camp Studio
Printed and bound in China by C&C Offset Printing Co., Ltd

MIX
Paper | Supporting responsible forestry
FSC www.fsc.org FSC® C008047

Thames & Hudson Australia wishes to acknowledge that Aboriginal and Torres Strait Islander peoples are the first storytellers of this nation and the Traditional Custodians of the land on which we live and work. We acknowledge their continuing culture and pay respect to Elders past and present.

TIWI IN PARIS

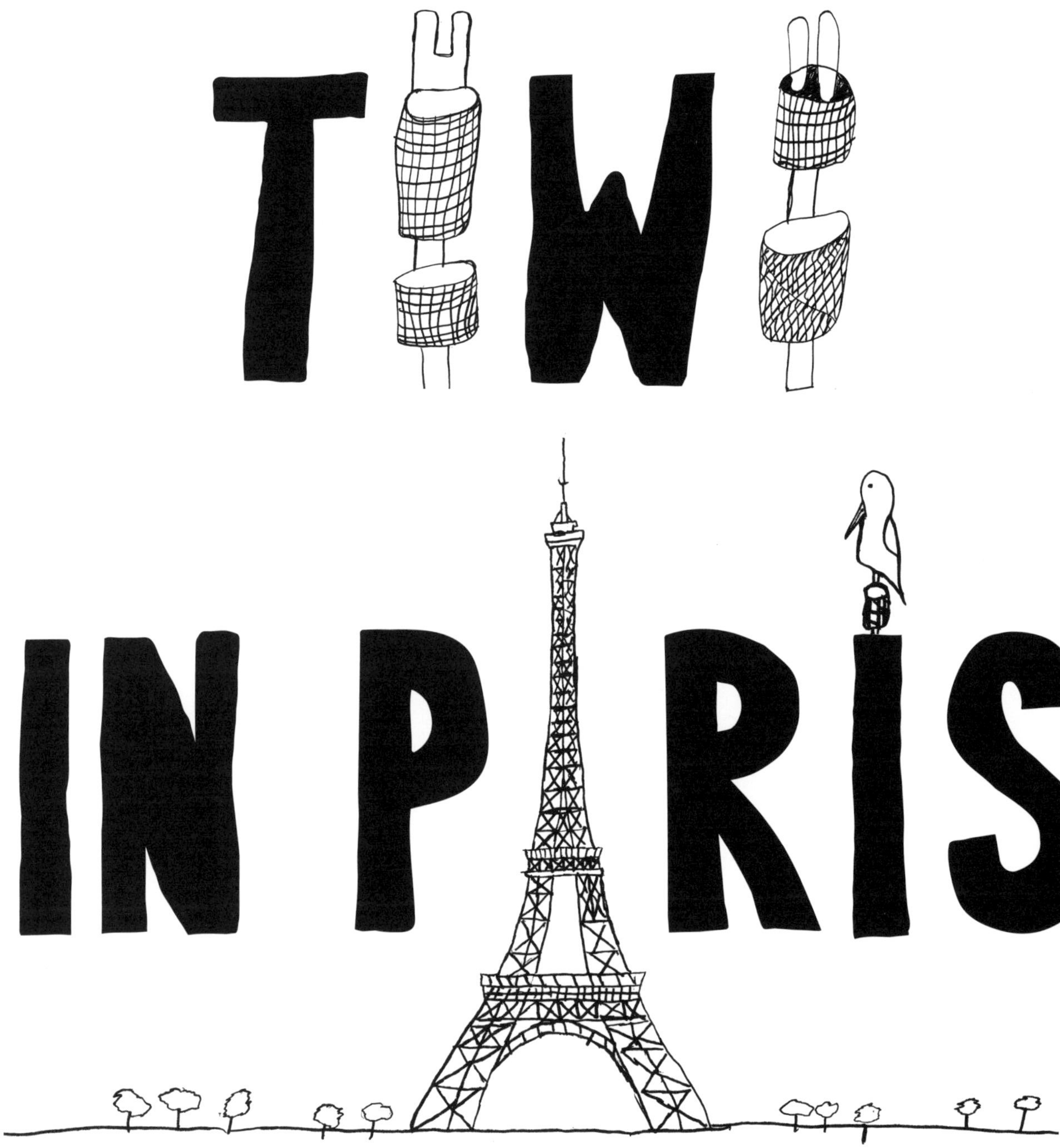

GLEN FARMER ILLORTAMINNI

The Tiwi Islands, also called **Ratuwati Yinjara**, are part of the Northern Territory in Australia, located approximately 80 kilometres north of Darwin, Larrakia Country.

The Tiwi Islands have been home to the Tiwi people since parlingarri (a long time ago). Just over 3000 people live on the islands and more than 90 per cent are Tiwi. It's a happy place, with strong families and strong culture.

Tiwi Islander people have a distinct language and culture and they are well known for their unique art, including painting, sculpture, fabric and jewellery. There are five art centres on the islands.

Find out more at tiwilandcouncil.com

My name's Glen Farmer Illortaminni
and I'm telling my story. Once I went to Paris as an
interpreter for the old fella, the famous artist named
Timothy Cook. He's my uncle and he was having
a show in Paris.

It was October when we went on that trip…

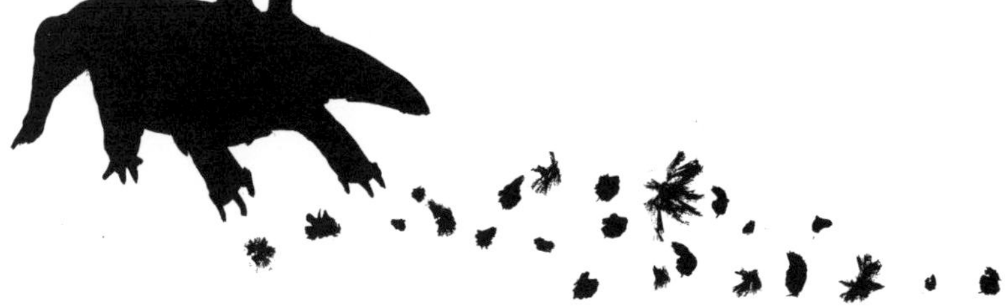

It was hot in the Tiwi Islands, build-up time. In the build-up, the yellow kapok flowers are on the trees telling us that the possums, stingrays and bandicoots are fat.

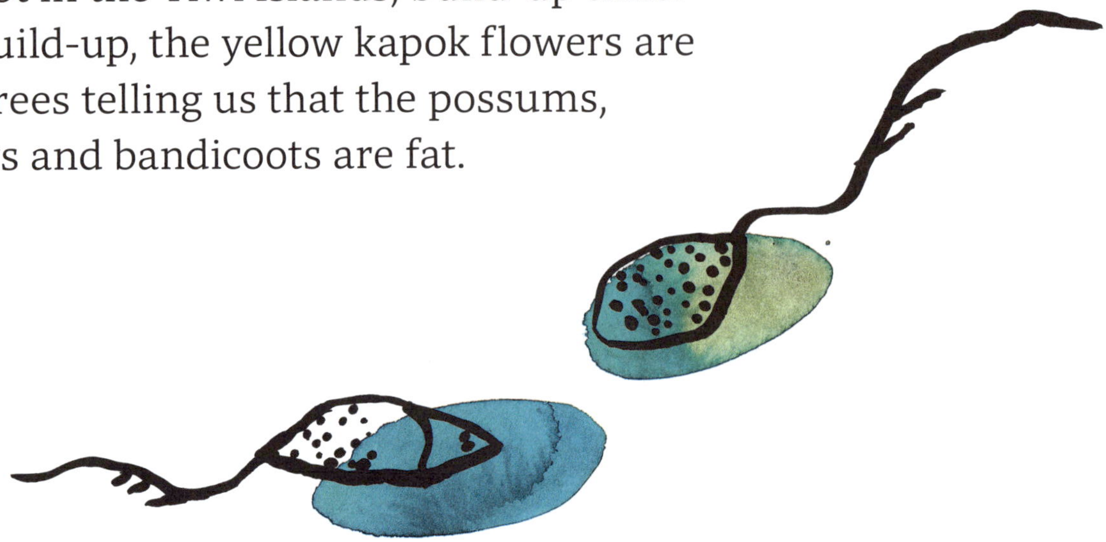

We follow the bees and collect bush honey.

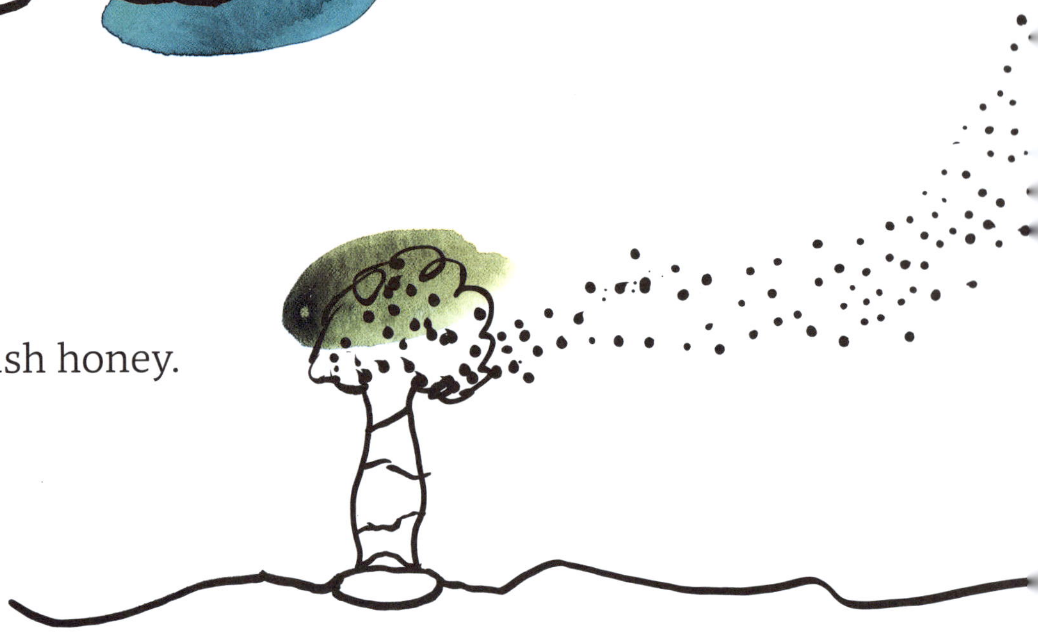

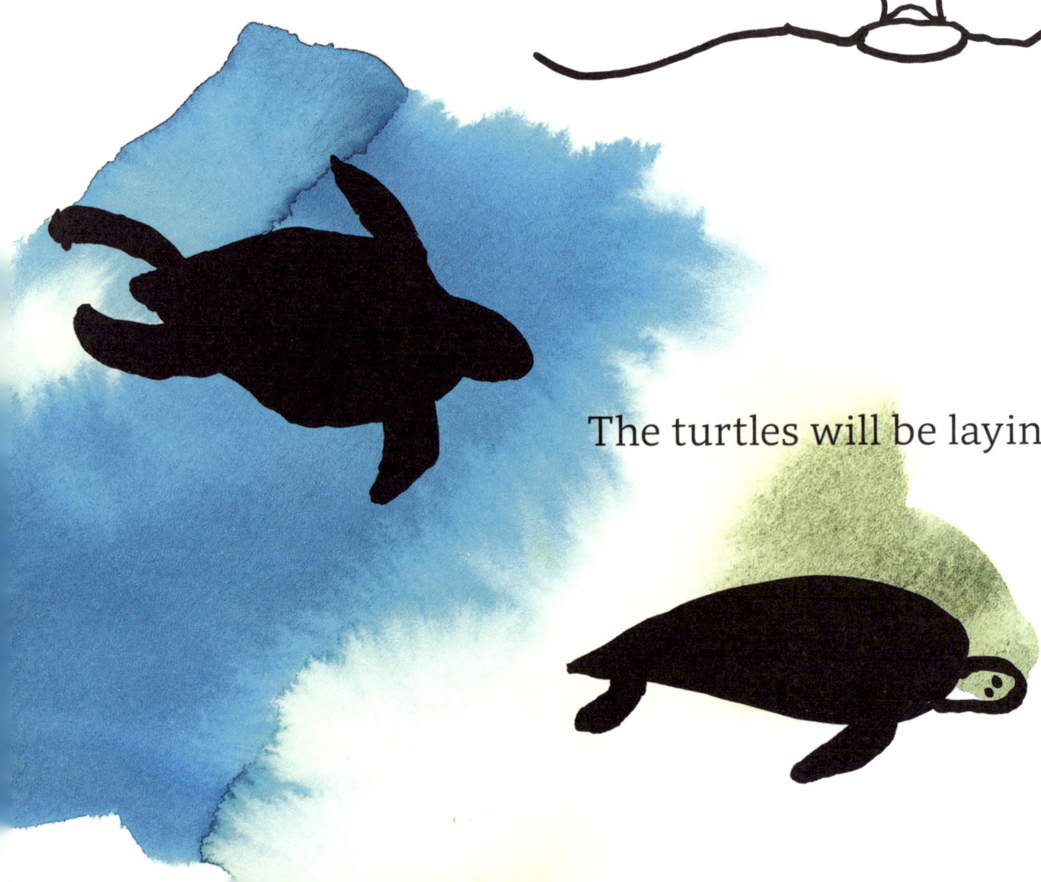

The turtles will be laying their eggs soon.

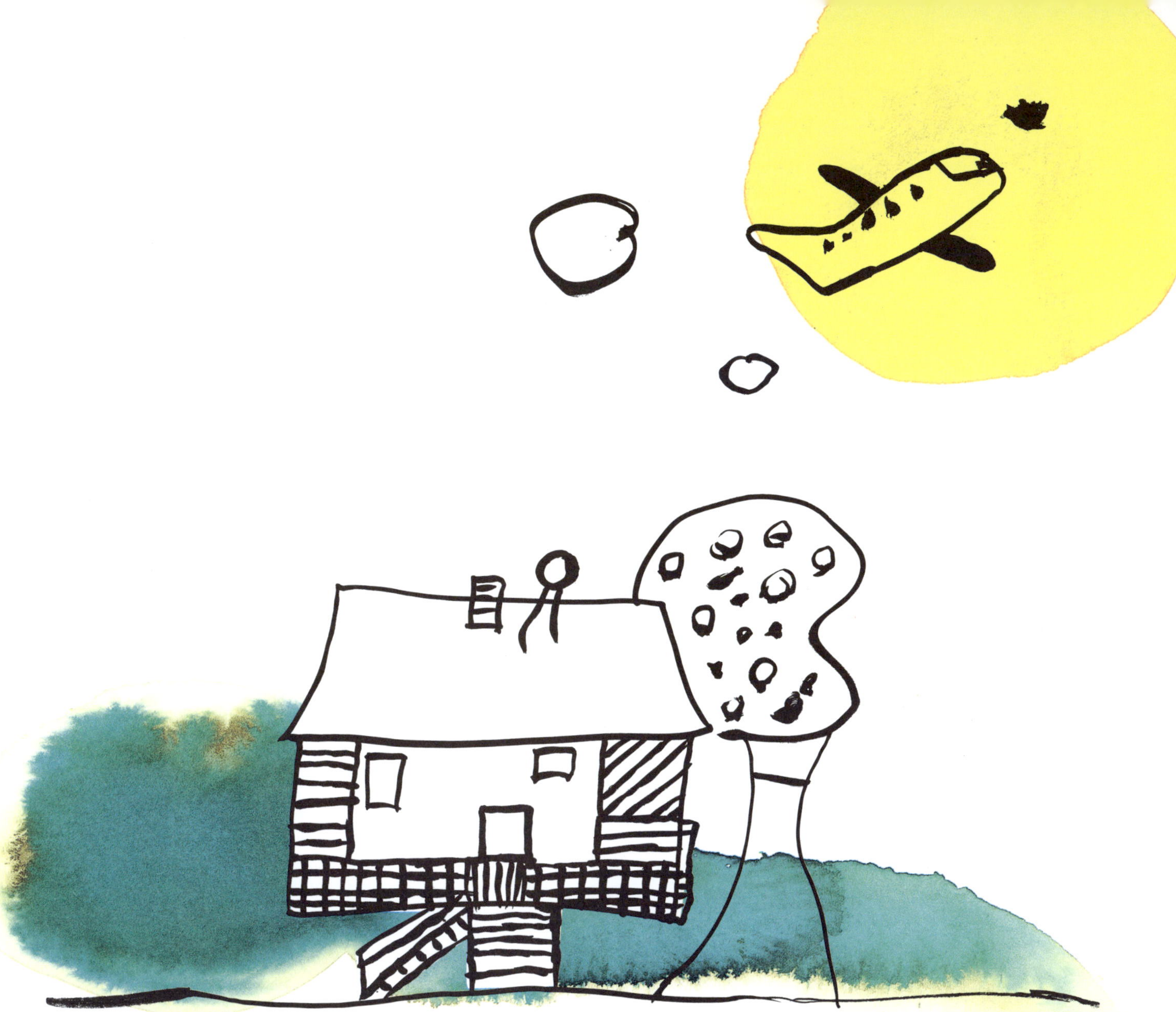

We left our home and flew to Paris.

We arrived in the afternoon and it was already getting dark.
We caught a taxi to our hotel then we walked out to dinner.
We ate frogs' legs, snails and spaghetti.

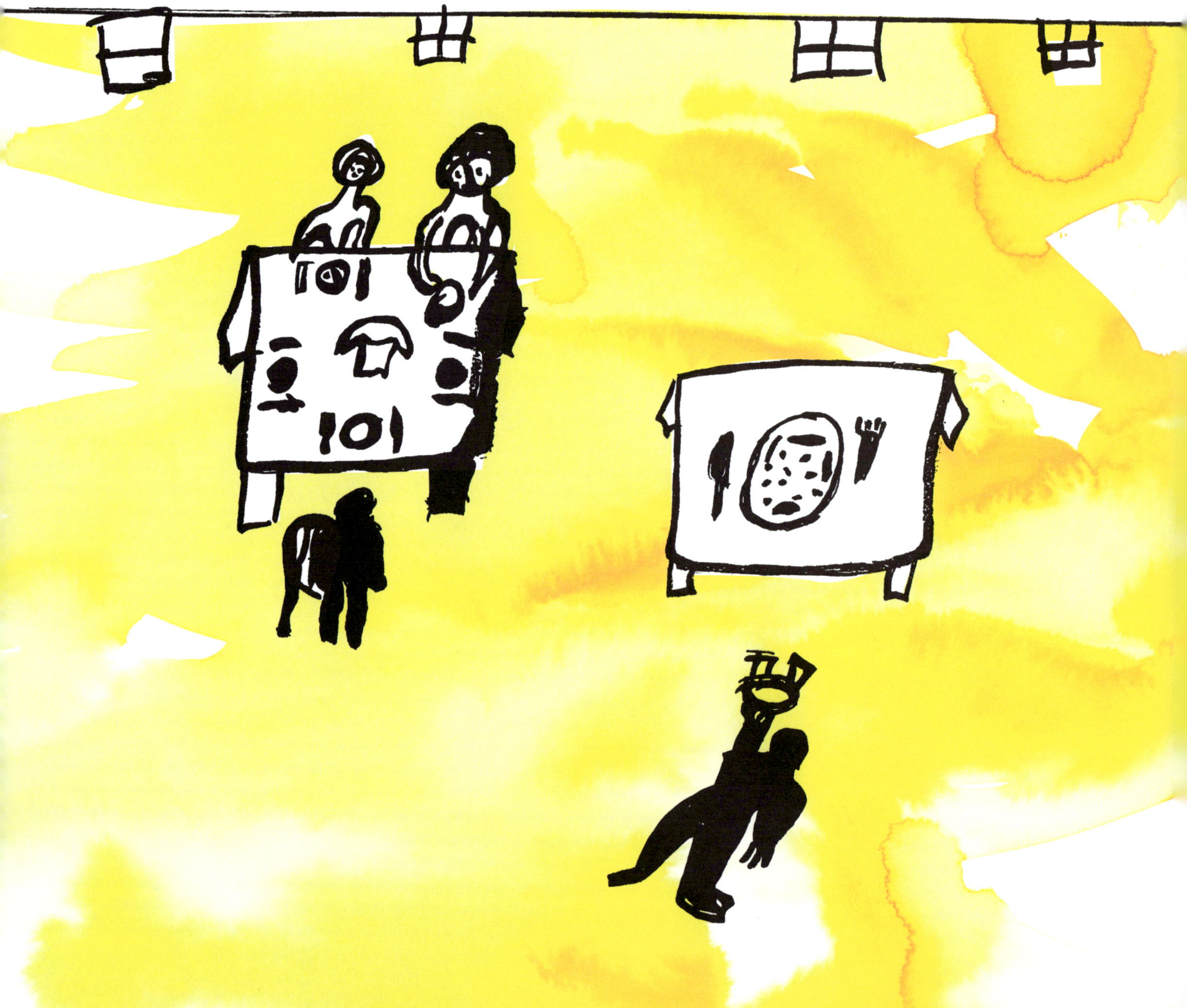

That night I couldn't sleep so I went for a walk.
All I took was a fifty euro note. I left my key at the desk.
I didn't tell anyone, I just ducked out and went to explore.

I was excited to see Paris and I thought I was going to come back, but I went too far… I was lost.

Lost in Paris.

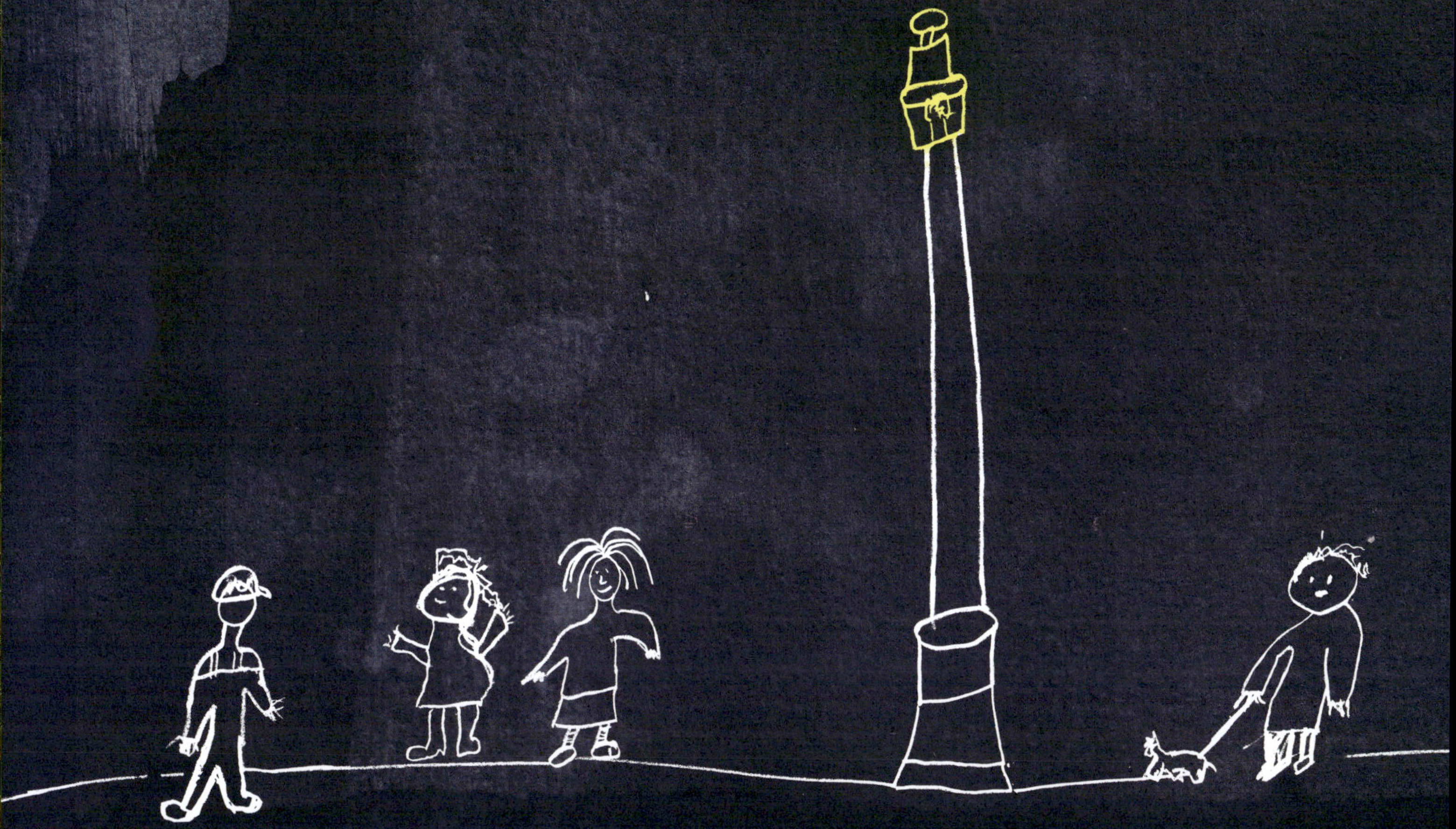

I walked for hours, talking to people,
but they couldn't understand me. I went to many hotels.
'I'm looking for Timothy Cook,' I said.
But nobody knew him.

I spoke English. They spoke French.
Nobody spoke Tiwi.

It was cold. It was very cold and I was very tired. I wanted to sleep and I remembered the airport was nice and warm and there were big comfortable chairs.

I knew the metro could take me there because I've watched the Jackie Chan movie *Rush Hour 3* about fifty times and it's filmed in Paris.

I went down into the metro and a kind lady gave me a ticket.

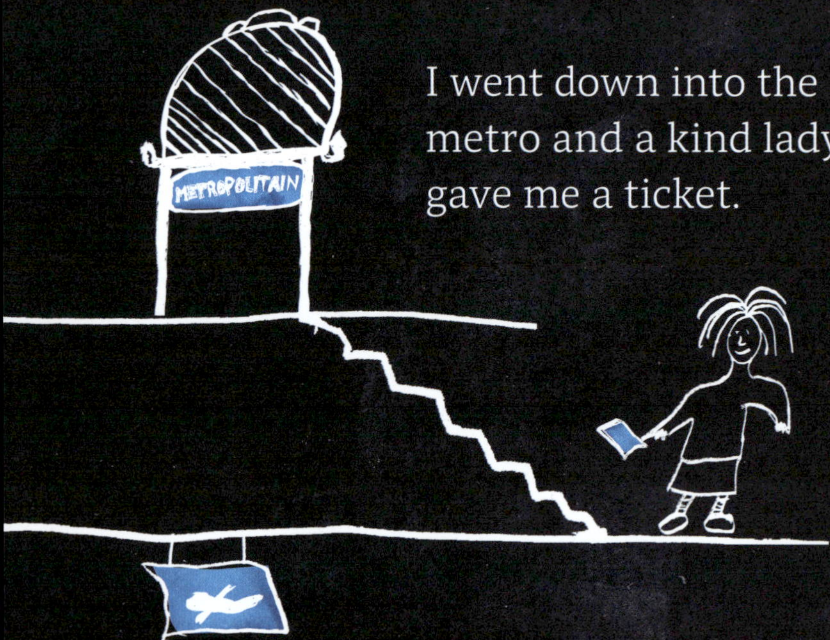

I saw the little blue airport sign so I followed it.

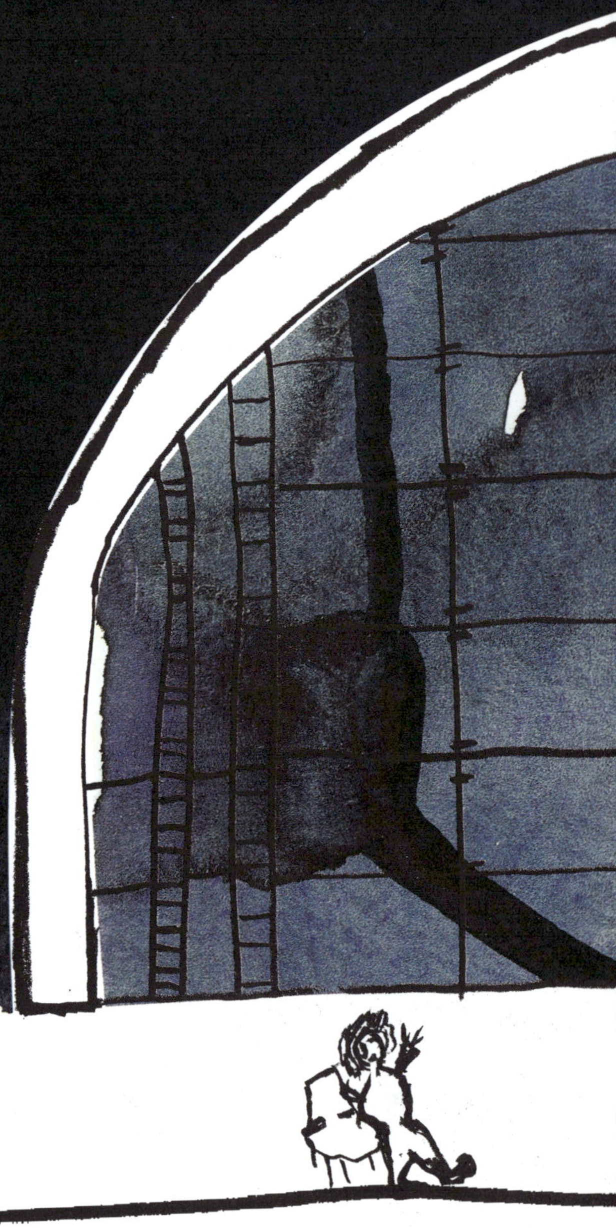

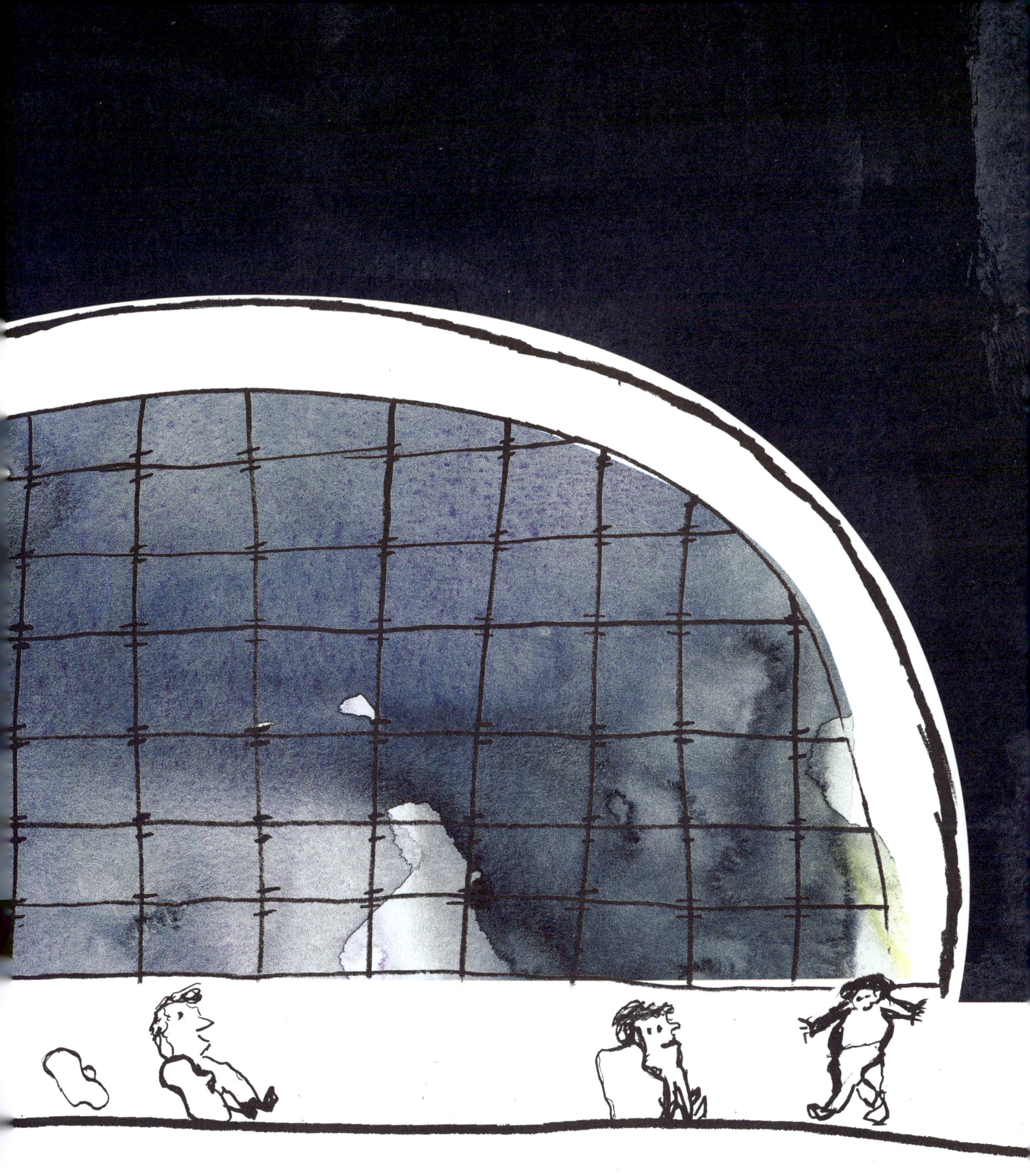

I slept at the airport on that comfortable chair
but police came with dogs. They told me to move on.

It was really late.

I was cold and it was raining.

And I was thinking, where am I gonna stay tonight?
I stopped for a while with some people who were sitting around a fire they'd made in a big drum.

They had an old couch there and they had nowhere to go. They were kind and I stayed with them for a while, but I was in a hurry.

I had to find the way back.

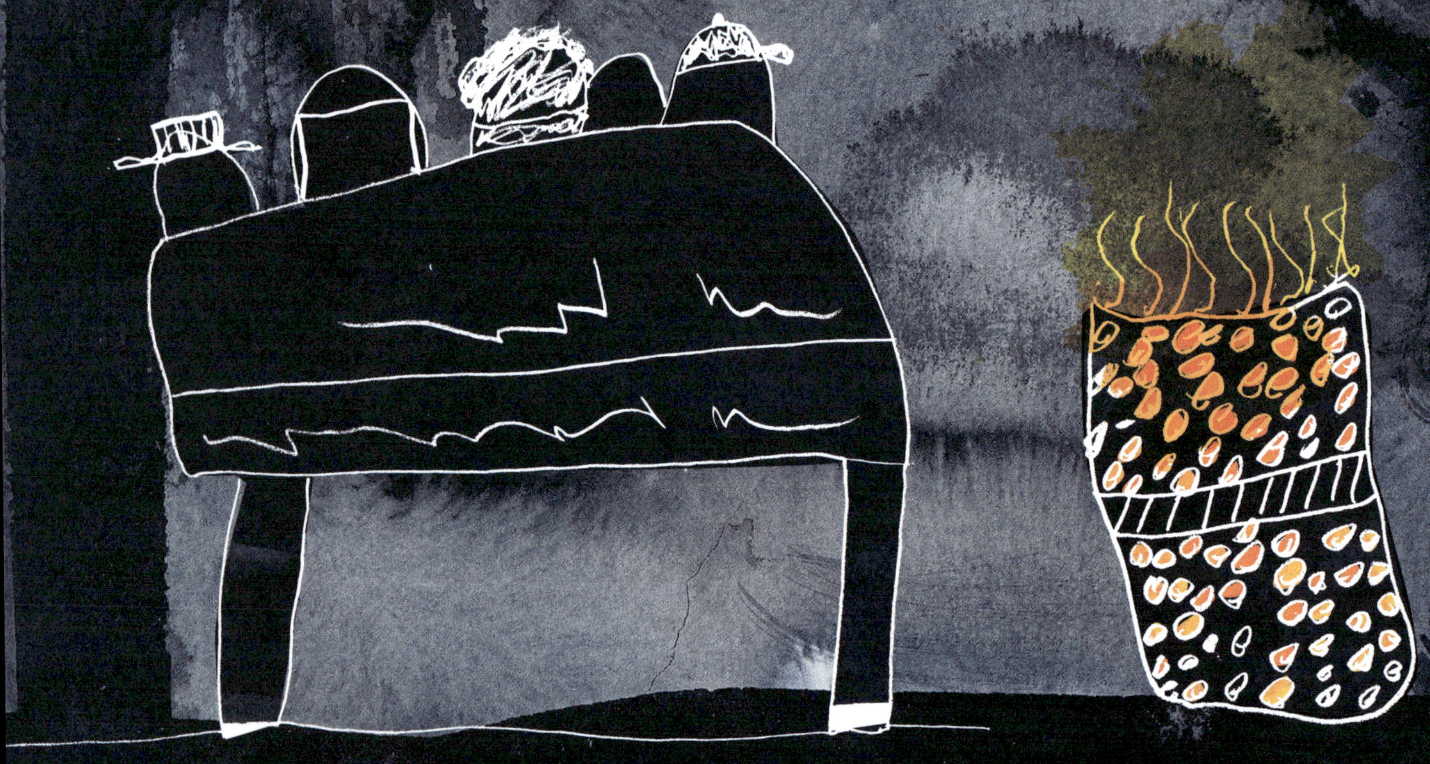

I walked and I walked and I walked.
Then I came to a huge vegetable market
like the ones in Darwin. They were selling all
kinds of food. There was cheese, fish, meat.

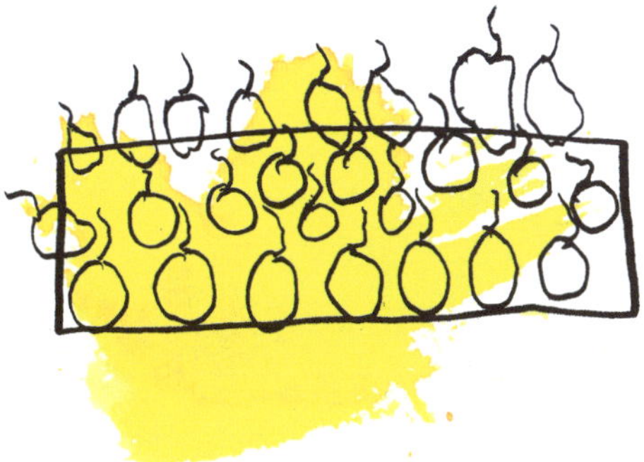

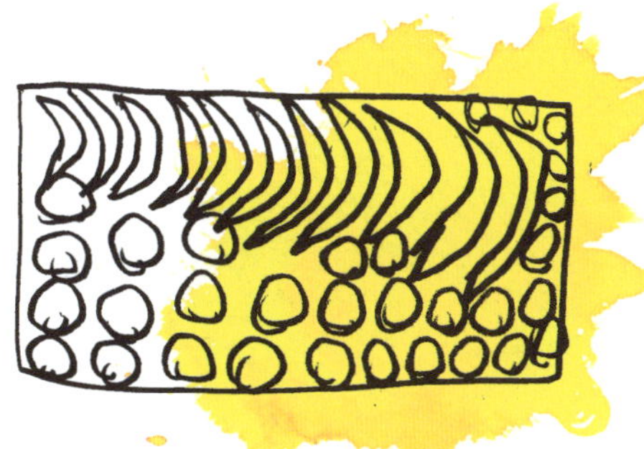

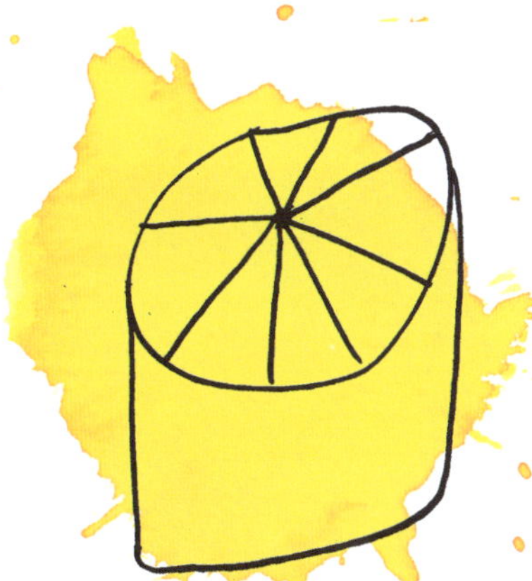

Someone gave me some
cheese on a little stick but it
was too strong.

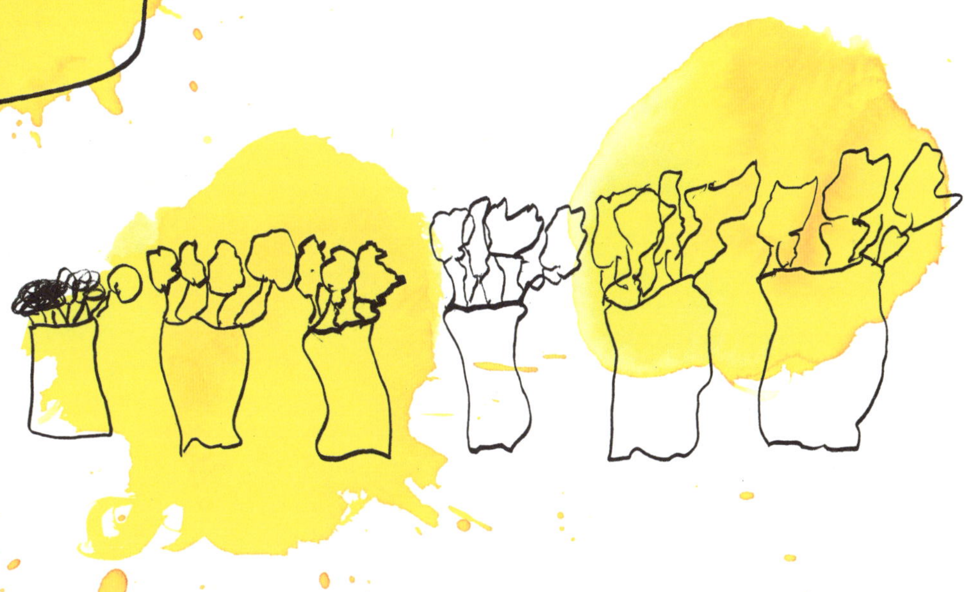

There were yellow flowers that reminded me of kapok flowers.

I wondered if I would ever get home.

Outside it was getting light and I needed to keep moving. The street was very wet – the river had flooded and people with big brooms were swooshing the water away.

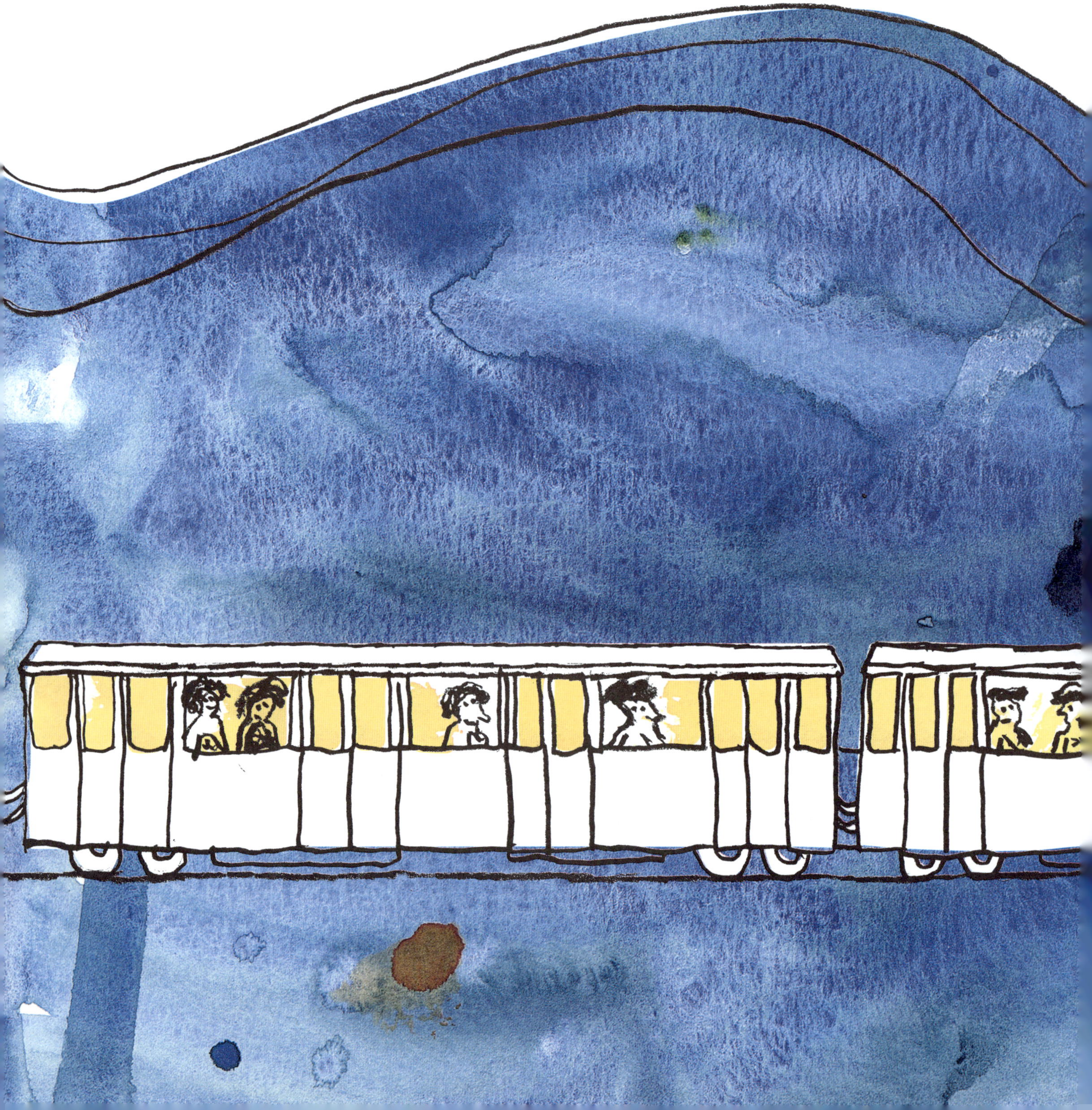

I saw another metro sign, followed the people down the stairs and slipped through the barrier behind a lady in a blue party skirt. When lots of people got off the train I got off too. I followed them and came to a canal.

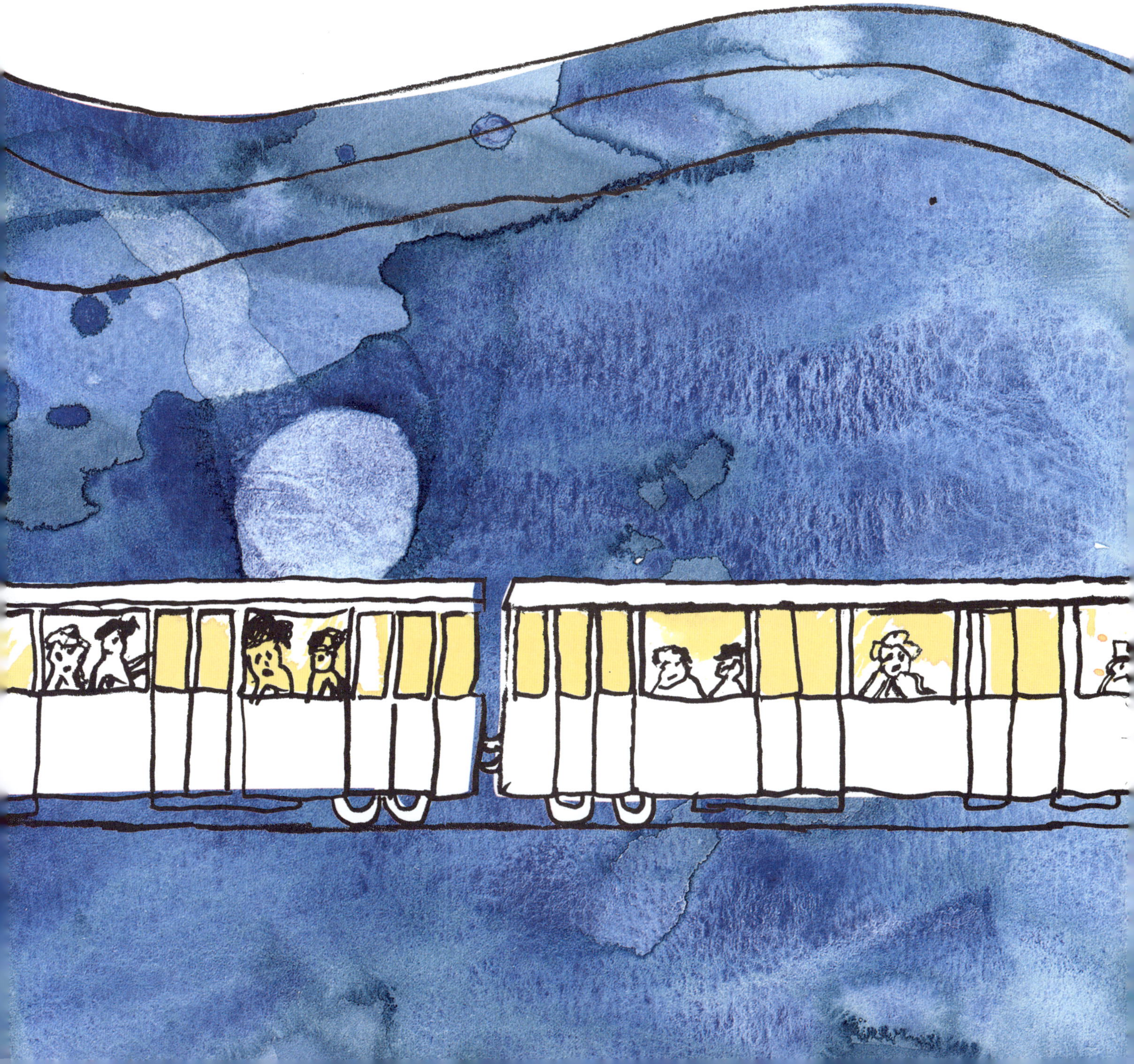

I walked until I got to a beautiful big building. There was a wide path leading up to that building, and craftsmen had spread out blankets. They were selling statues of the Eiffel Tower and they asked me if I wanted to buy one.

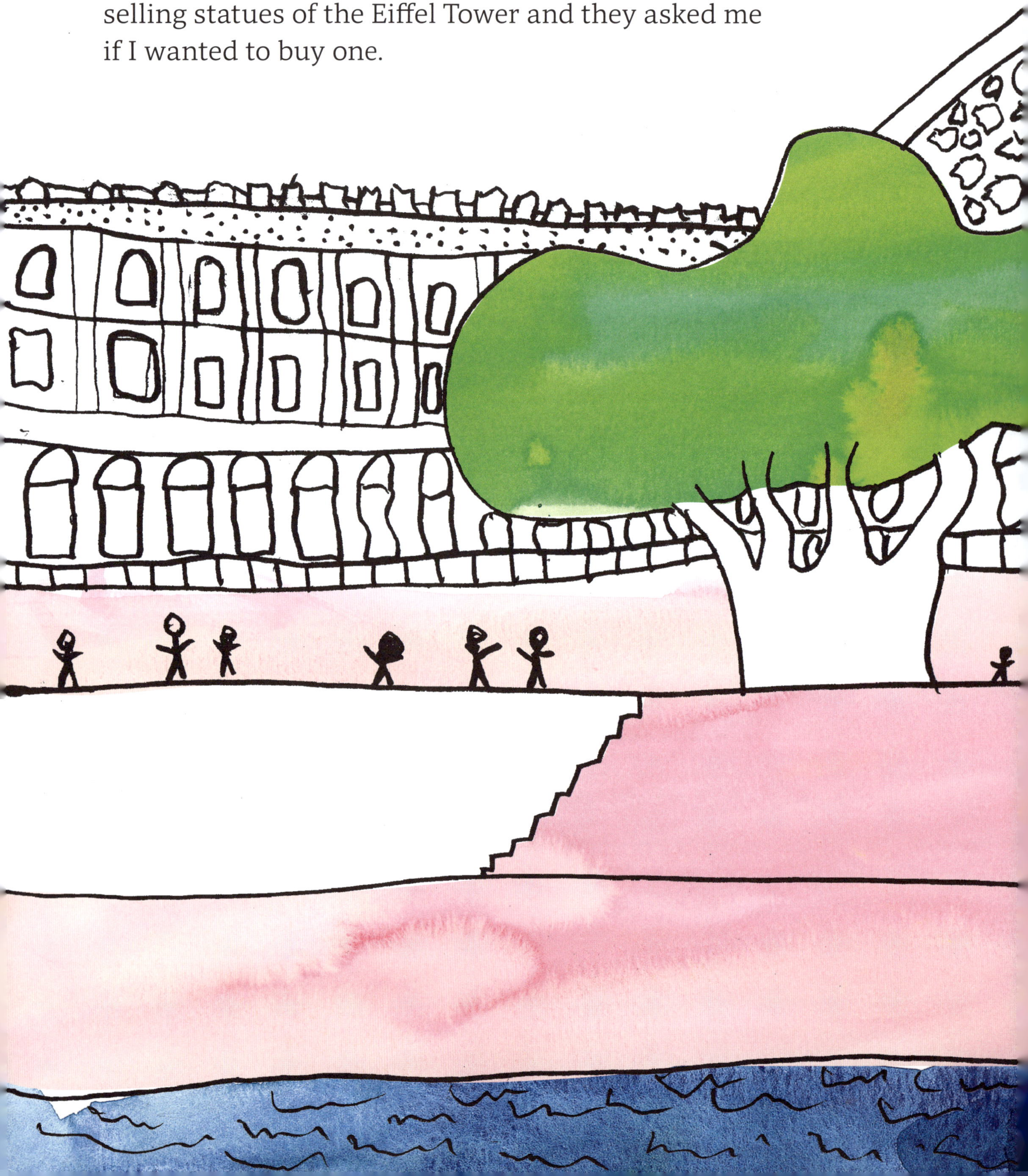

'No!' I told them. 'I am lost and I have no money.' They gave me one instead. They thought I was joking, but I told them, 'No, I'm not mucking around.'

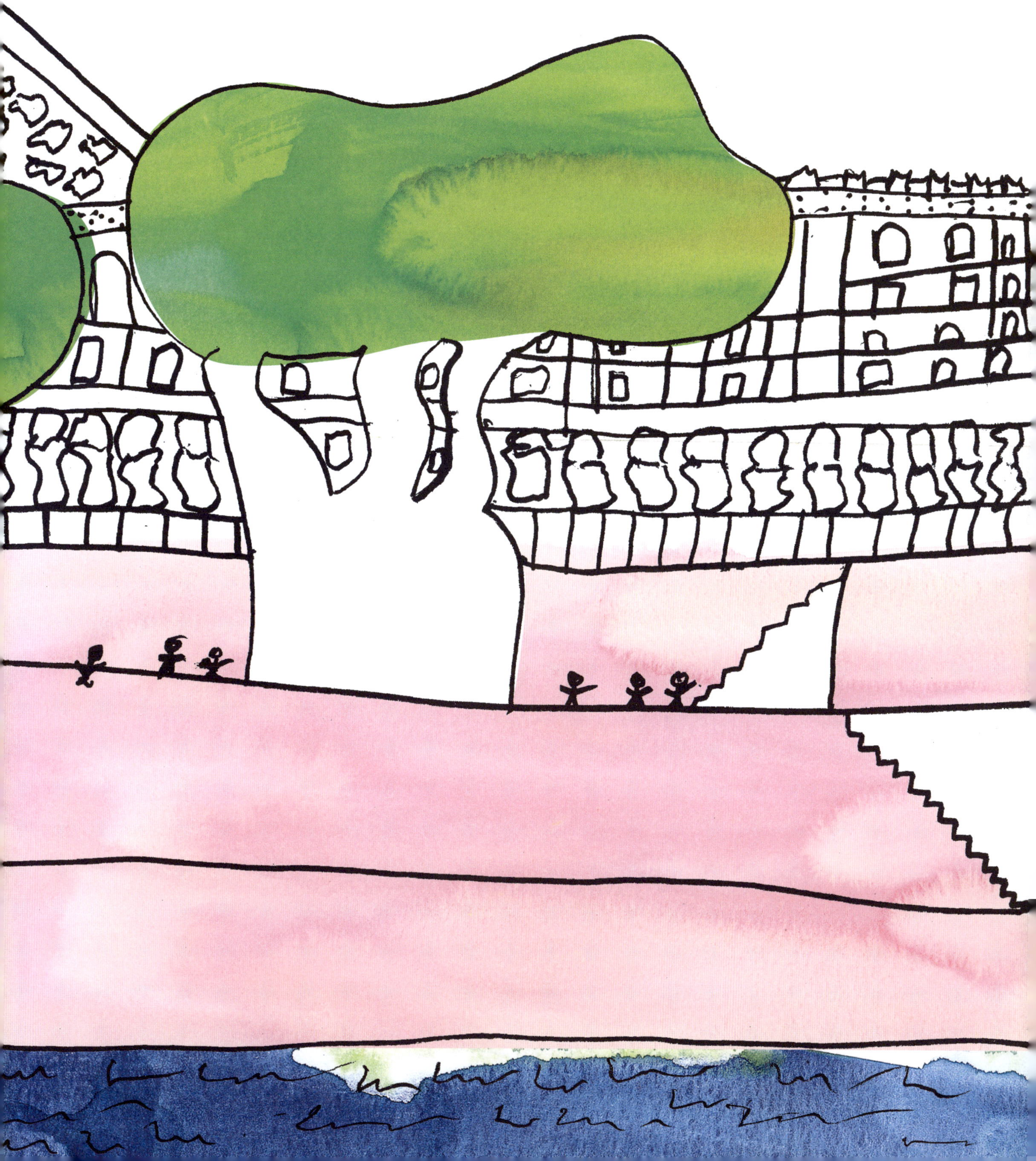

A tour guide walked past with a group of tourists and he was speaking in English. He was talking about olden times when the German army was trying to take over Paris because Hitler was the ruler. I decided to walk along behind them. I heard about that for a long time.

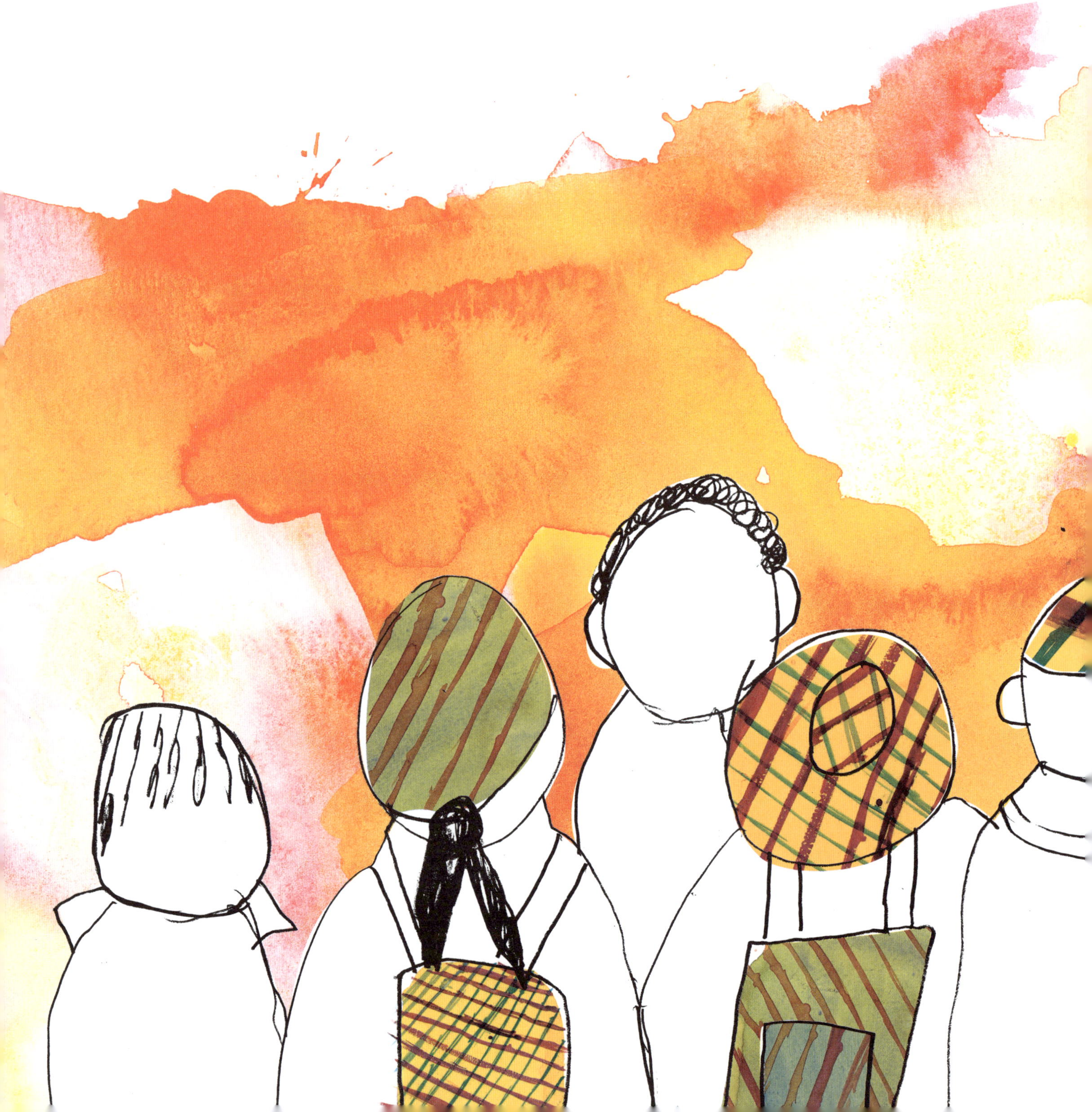

That guide was talking, but he was looking at me too, and laughing. But I didn't laugh. When I work at the art centre, I'm the cultural liaison, so I knew not to laugh. That's a serious story.

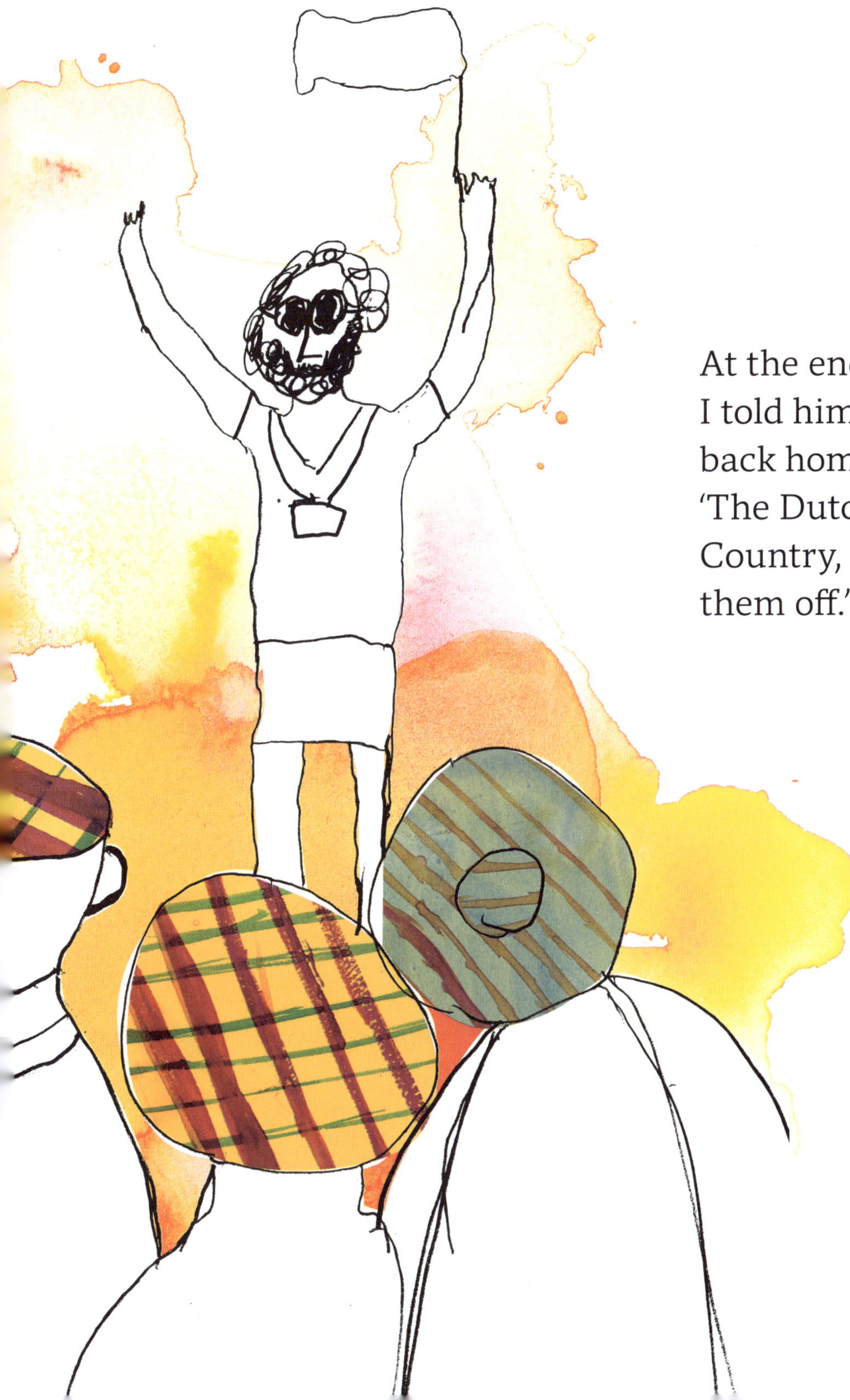

At the end of the tour
I told him about being a guide
back home. Then I told him,
'The Dutch came over to my
Country, but my people fought
them off.'

But when I told him
I was lost in Paris,
he didn't believe me.

I had never been so tired in all my life.
My feet were sore and I slipped on the wet footpath.
I hit my head and I got a big cut, it knocked me out.

I was lying there on the ground.
When I came to, I saw a little girl peering
out the window of her papa's café.

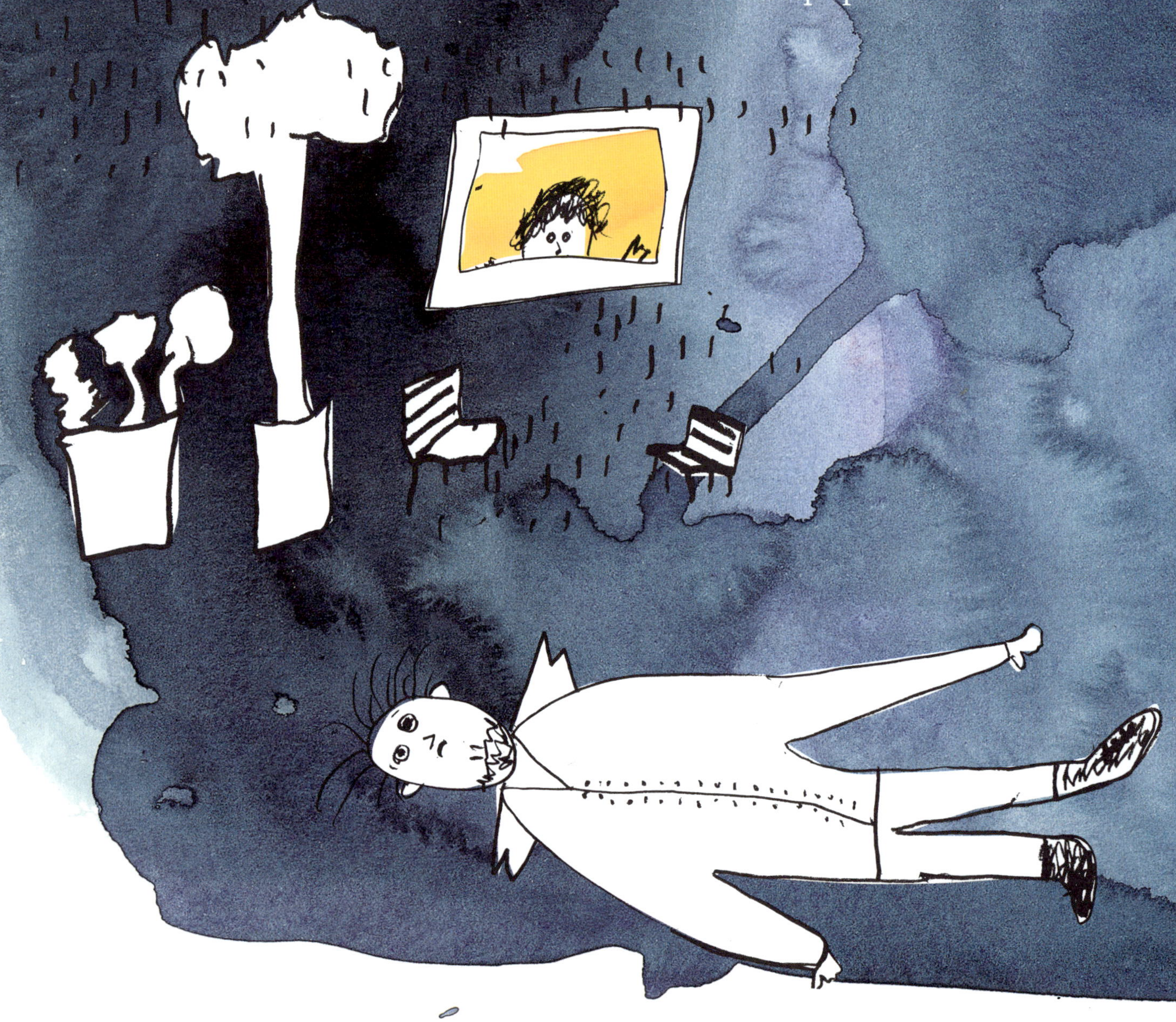

She saw that I was in trouble so she came out
and bent right down. She said, 'Bonjour.'
I think she was about five years old.

Her papa brought me inside and made me a nice hot cup of coffee. He gave me a baguette with ham and cheese. I was hungry and he was kind.

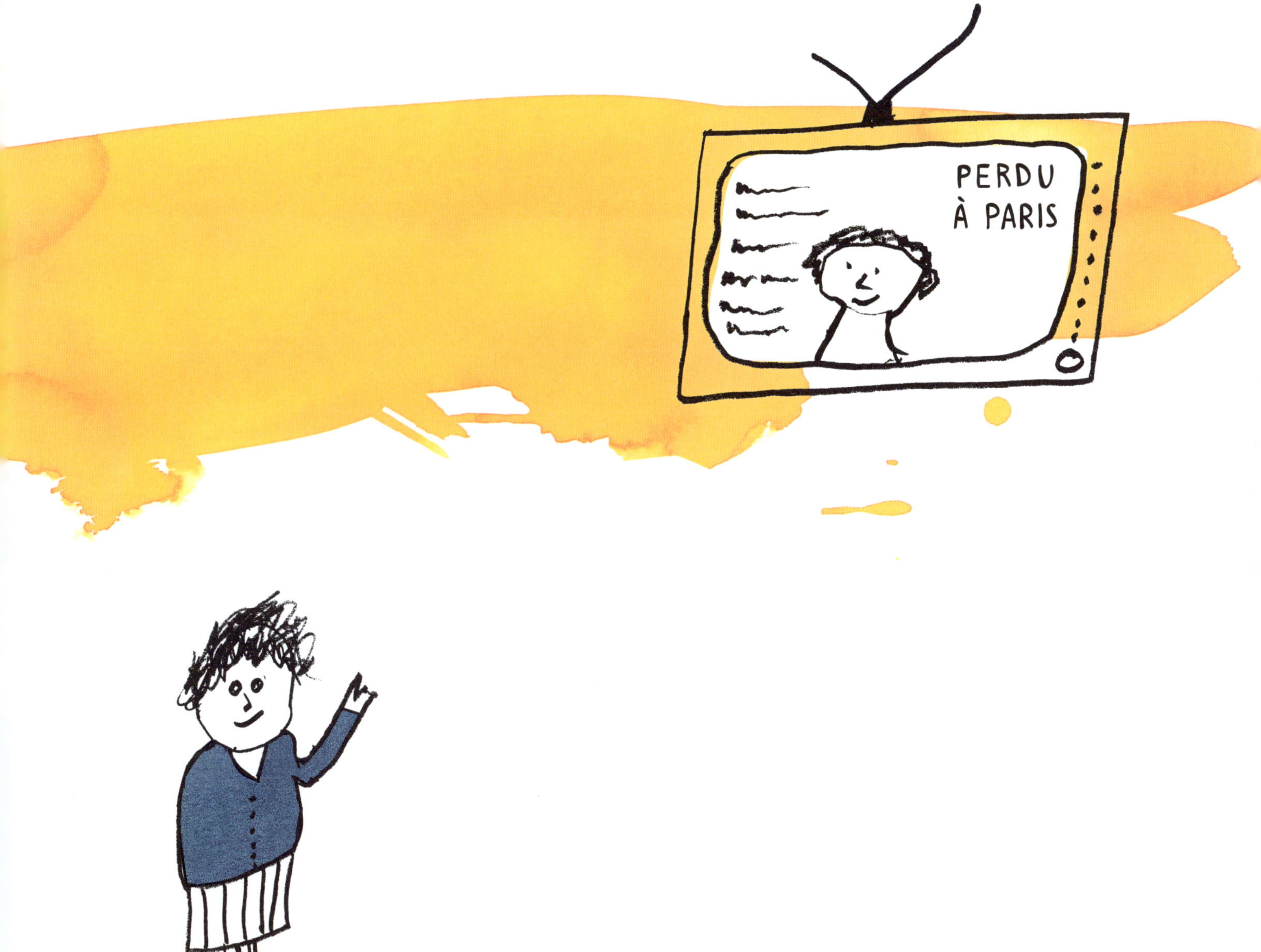

While I was eating, the little girl started to laugh. She pointed up at the TV in the corner and said something to her papa. And there I was.

I was on TV!

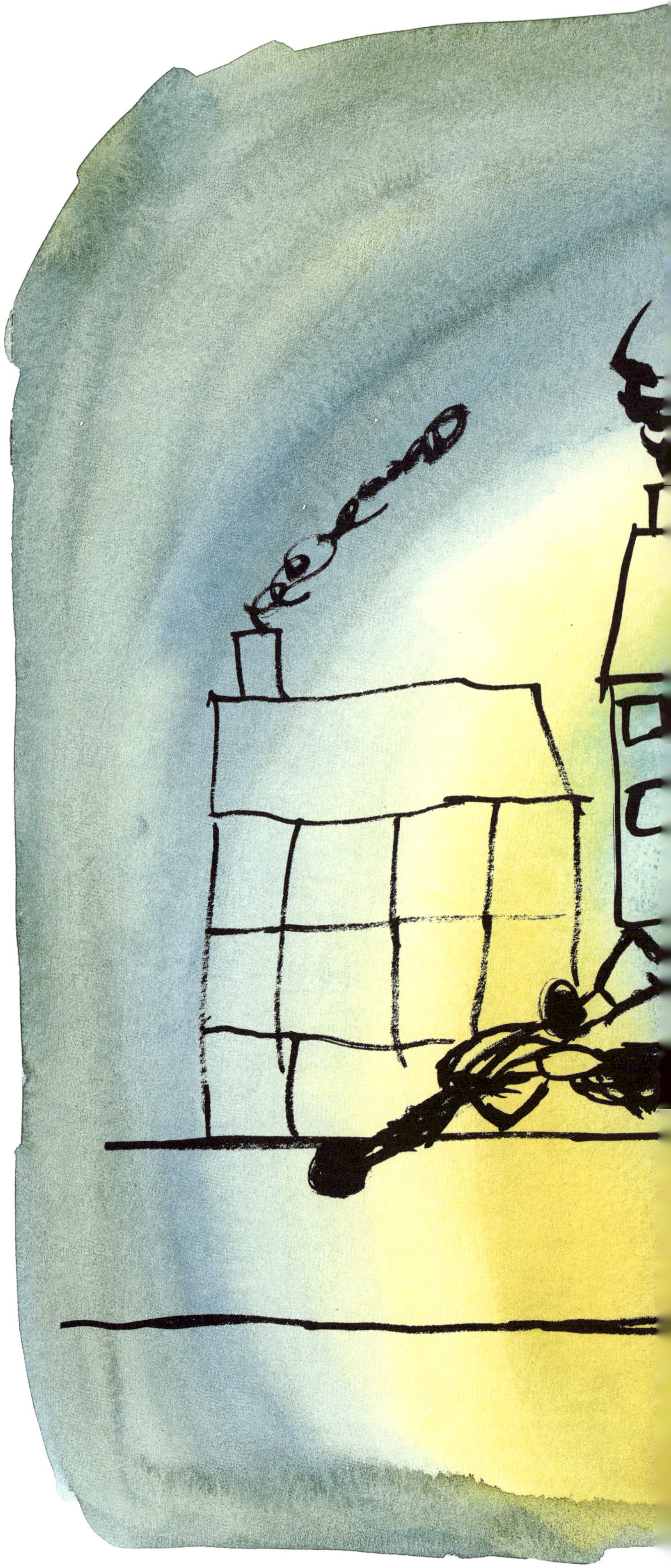

Soon an ambulance
arrived. I don't know,
perhaps that kind man
had rung them. They put
a bandage on my head and
drove me to the hospital.

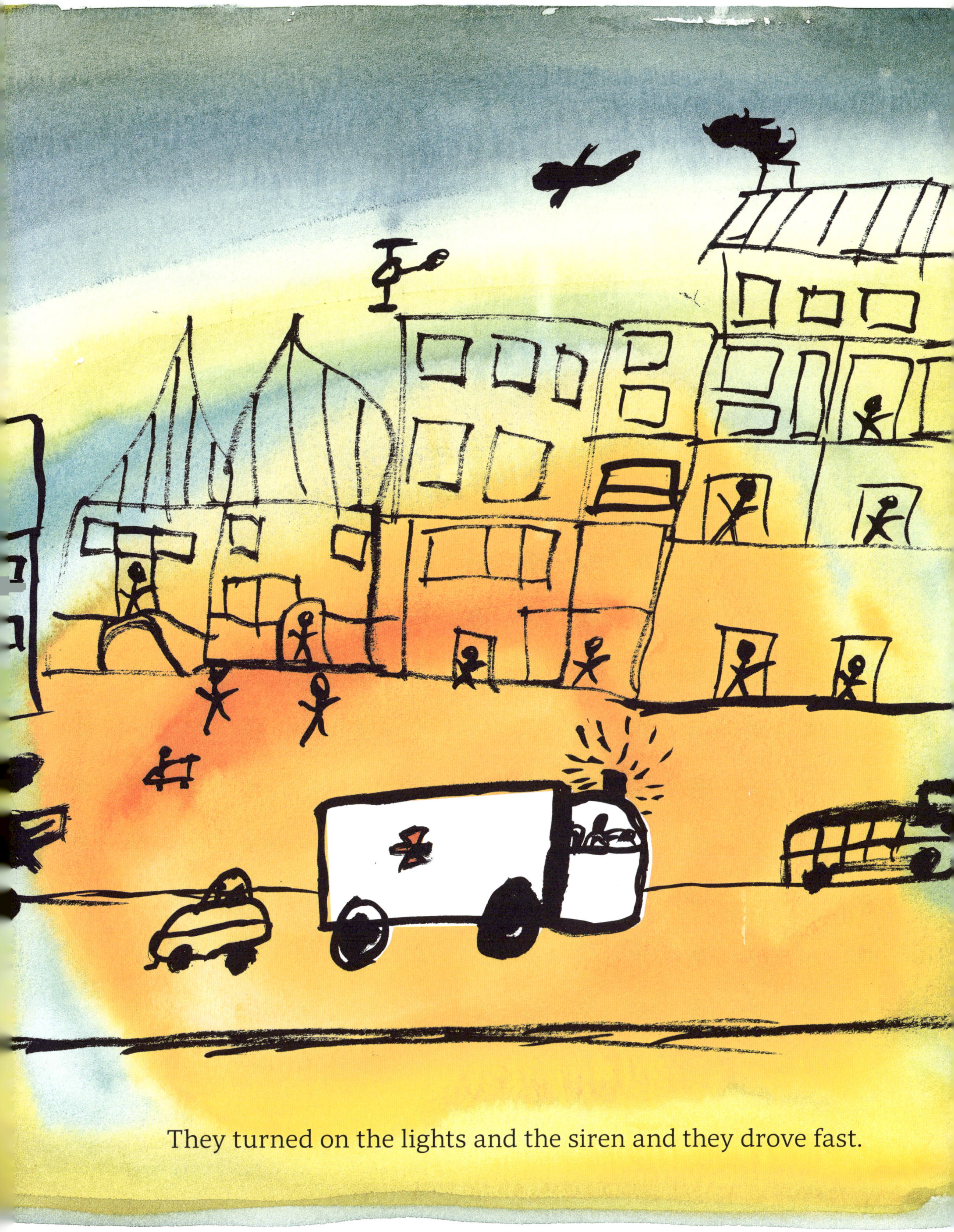

They turned on the lights and the siren and they drove fast.

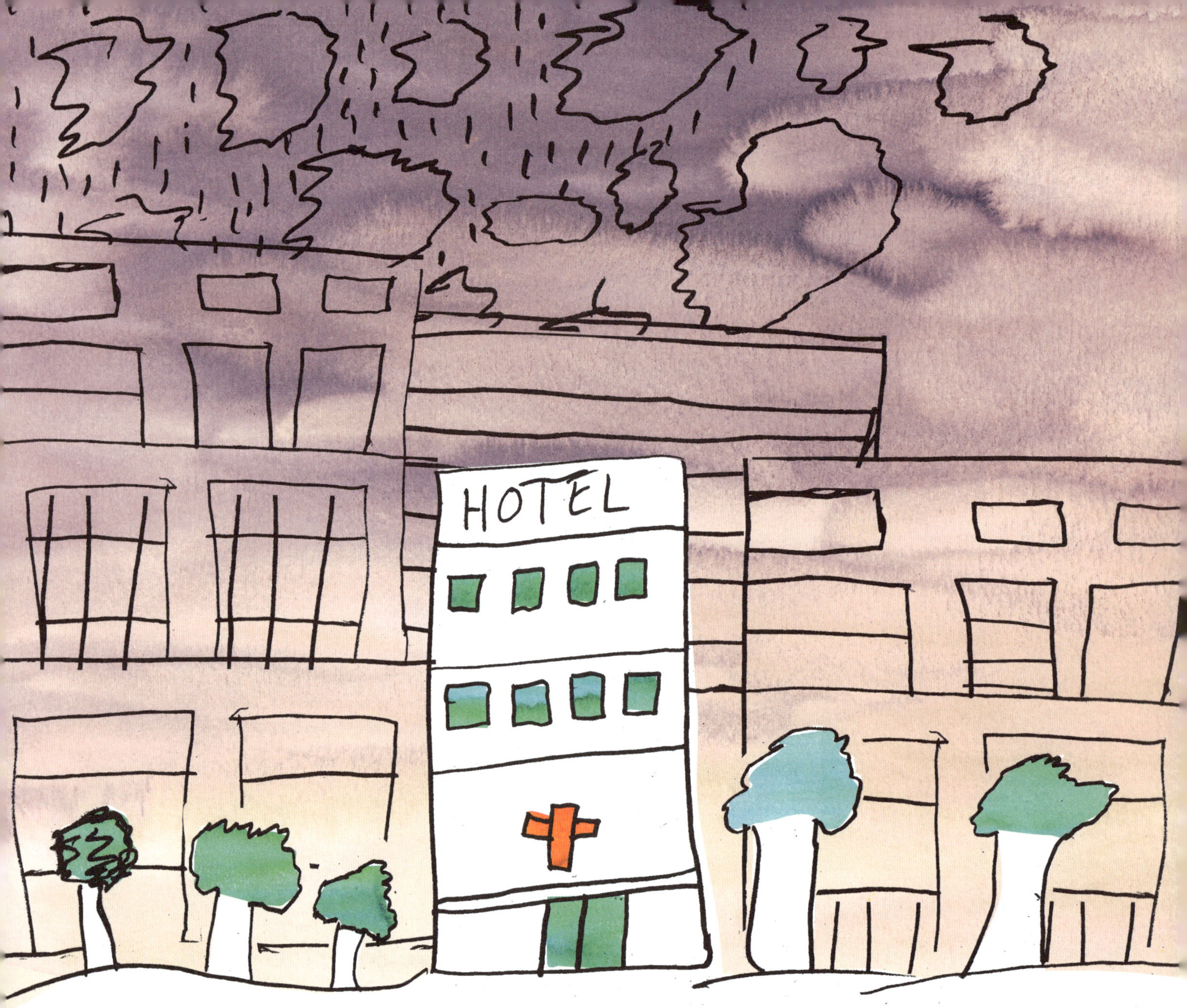

Later I found out that our hotel was straight above the hospital. Timothy was in the same building, but I didn't know.

They put some stitches in my head and
I asked them for some clean clothes.

They gave me a pair of green pants and a green
gown. They gave me some special shoes.
White plastic clogs that were very comfortable.

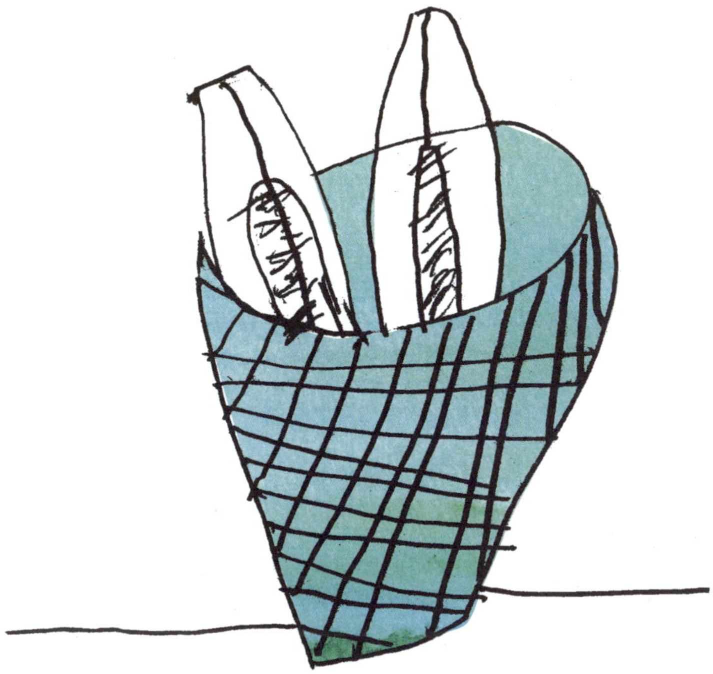

I threw my other shoes
in the bin. They were
rock'n'roll shoes that
I had bought in an op shop
in Darwin. They gave me
blisters so I threw them out.

It was warm in the hospital and I had a little snooze
but I was in a hurry. I had to find the others in case
I got left in Paris for good. So I left.

I took my jacket and I walked out of that place.

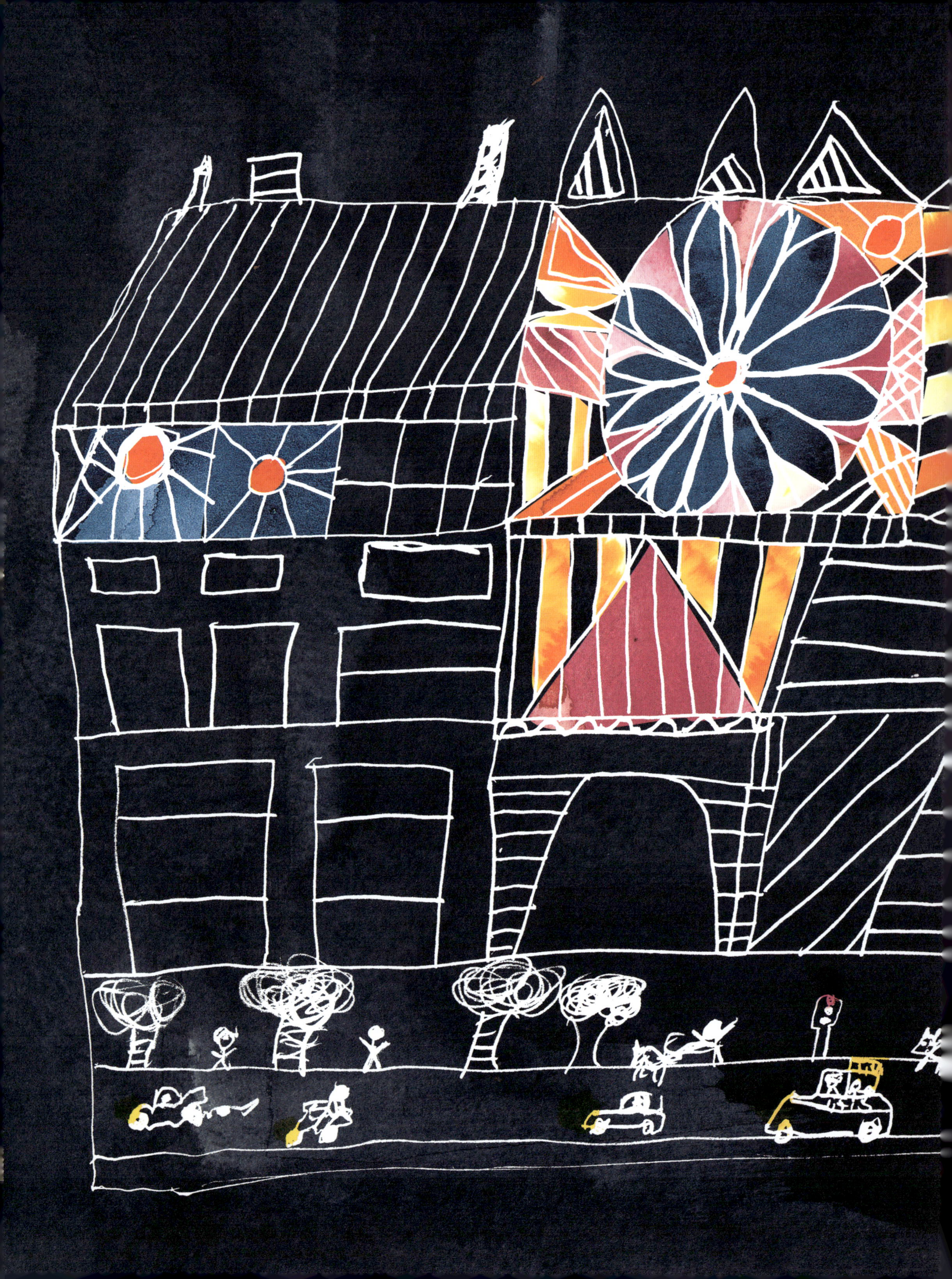

It was dark again and
I walked to a big church.
I was scared that
I would never get home.
I was lost and
I needed to pray.

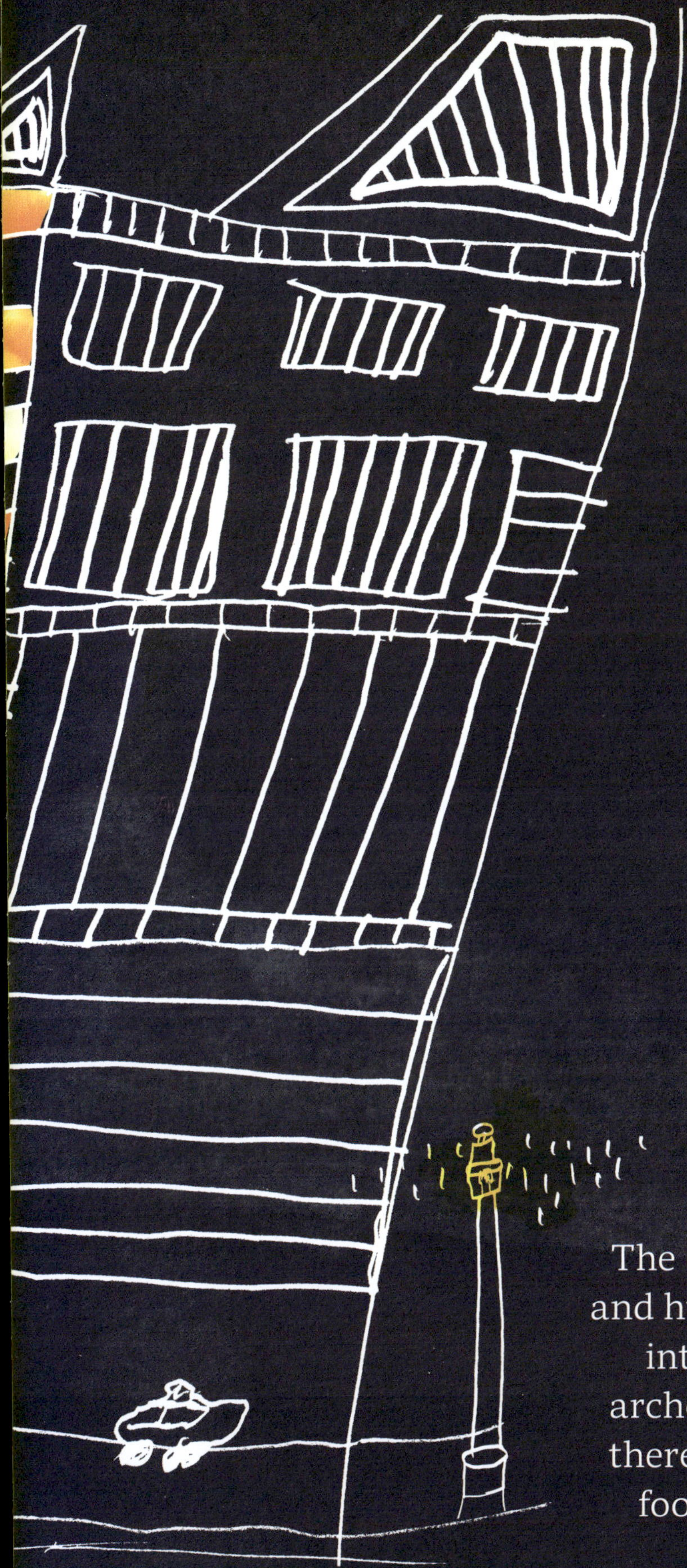

The church was an old, old building, and huge. There were monsters carved into the stone and big, colourful, arched windows. When I went inside there were people in there giving out food. They gave me a blanket and I had a sleep on a mattress.

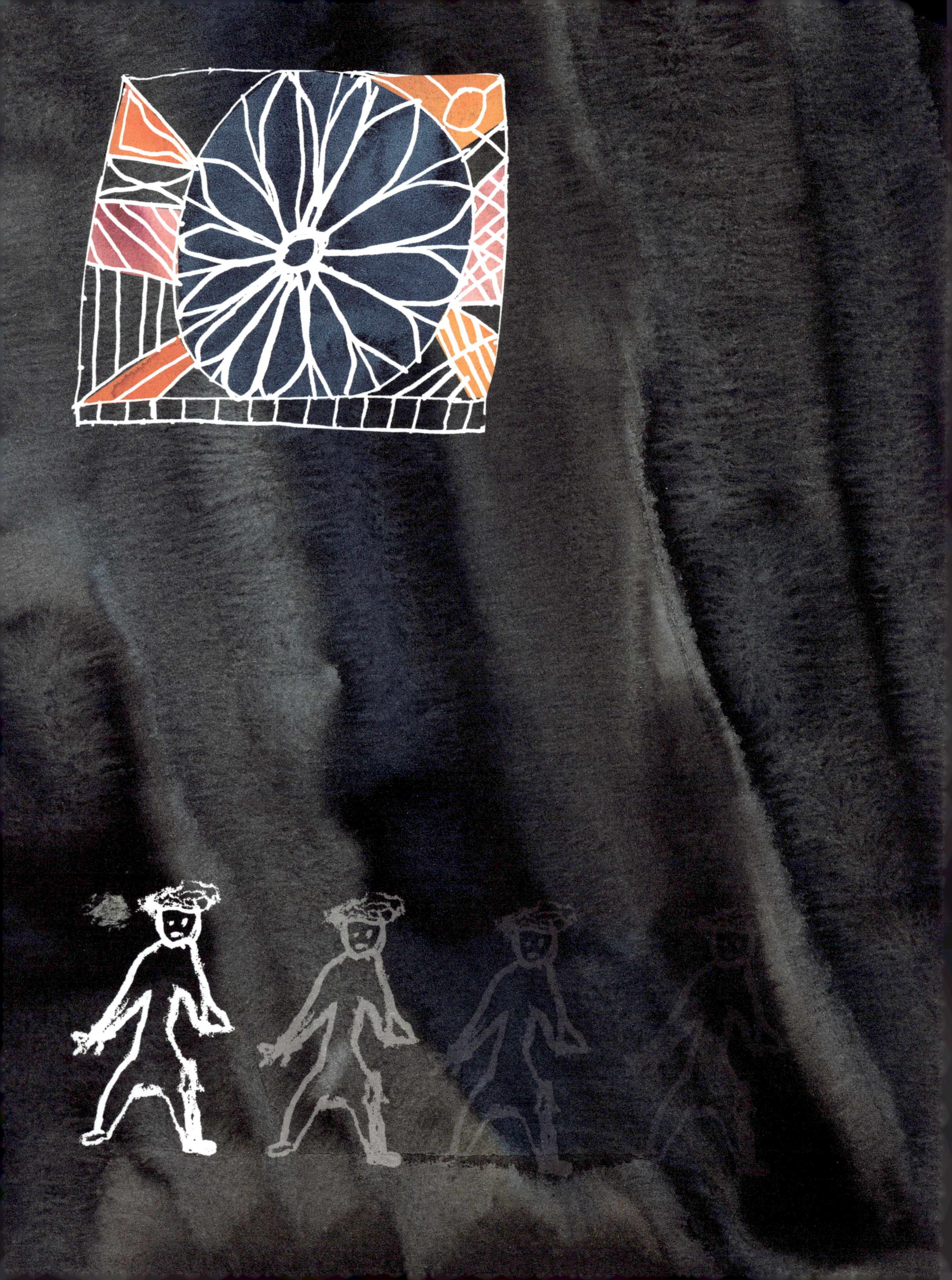

In the middle of the night I woke up.
A man who looked like a priest walked past.
He was wearing a white robe with a belt and
as I looked again he disappeared.

I felt a strong wind, and I knew it was a sign
that I needed to keep on the move.

Go! Go! I had to find the others or
I would be left behind.

I needed to get back to my Country and back to
my family. I prayed for my angel to take me home.
My middle name is Gabriel so I knew that my
angel would take me home. That's how come
I'm here telling this story.

The next day I walked and walked.
My feet felt better now, in those hospital
shoes, but the hospital pants were very thin.
They didn't keep the cold wind out.

I walked to a great big arch and I stood under
it and looked down a boulevard. It was very
beautiful. So was the Moroccan lady
I met there with her son.

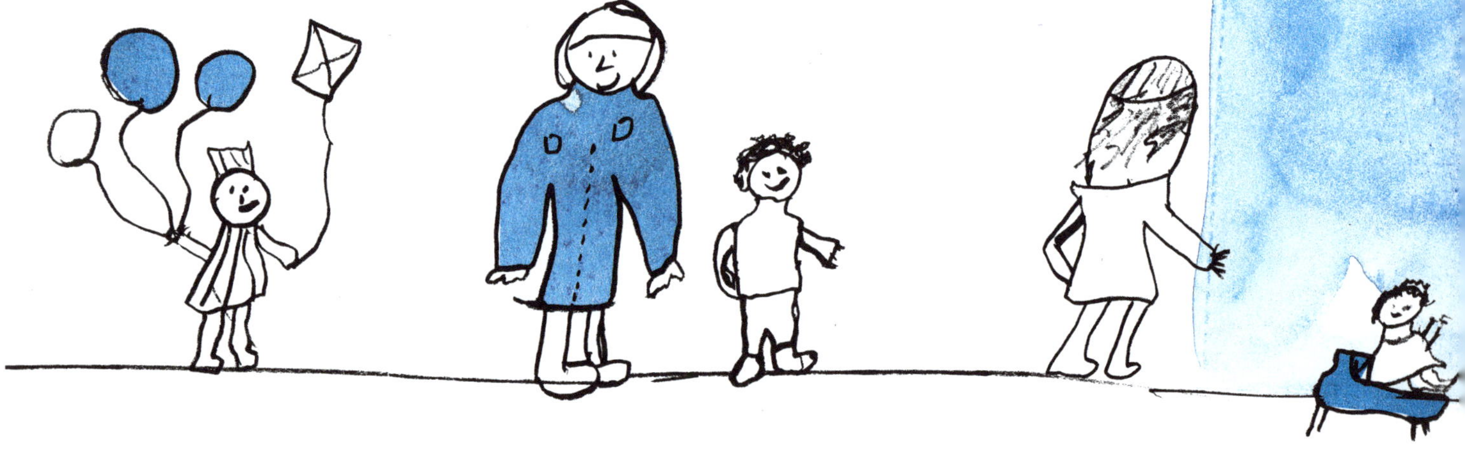

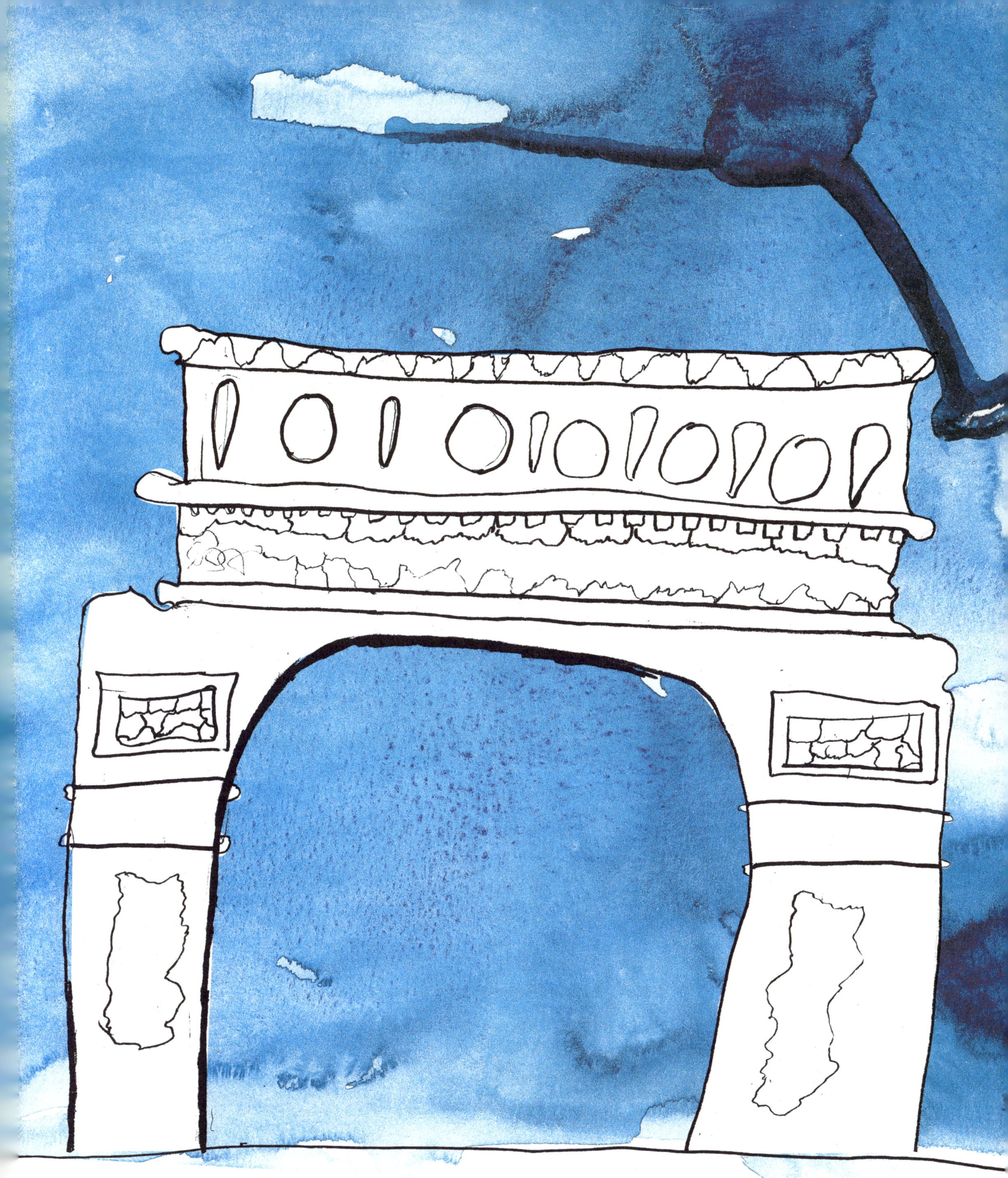

She asked me to go to her house and she made me some nice food. It was a hot chicken curry, with rice and lots of spices. It was delicious. I had never eaten food like that. I slept at her place that night, and she wanted me to stay longer, but I told her, 'No, sorry, I'm on a mission. I have to go.'

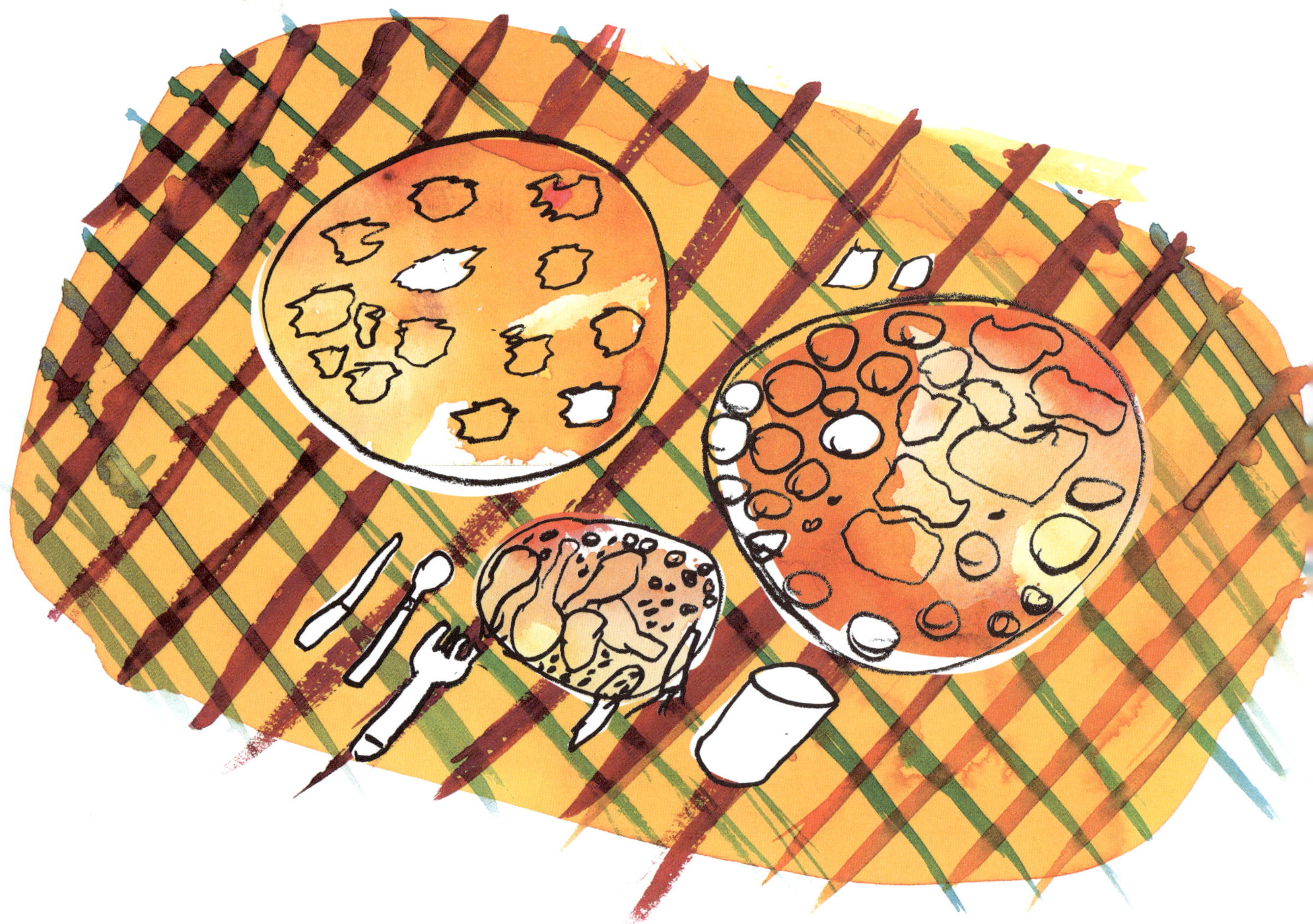

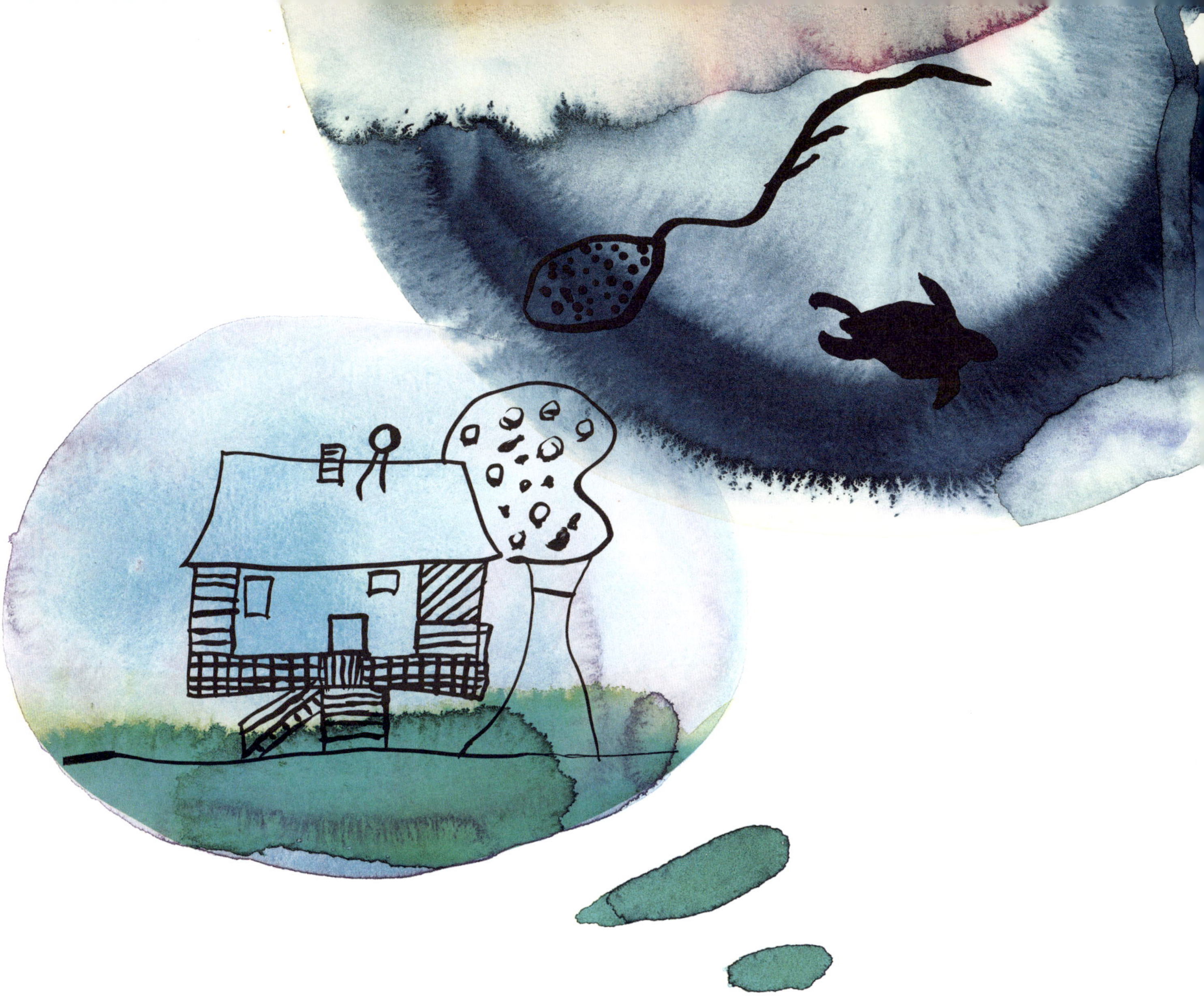

I had lost count of the days, and I wasn't sure when we were meant to be leaving. My mind was all over the place, but I felt my Countrymen beside me, willing me to come home.

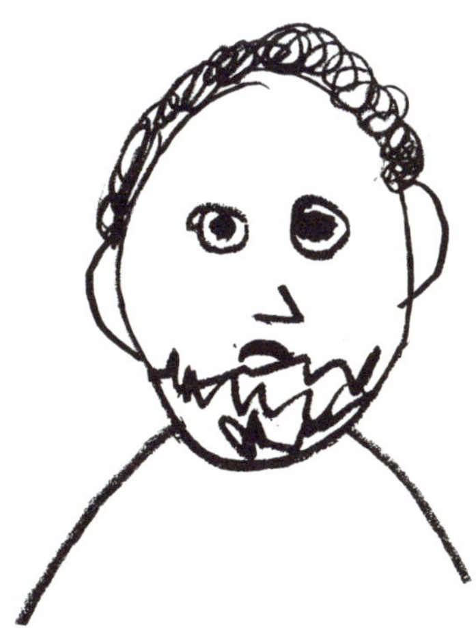

I needed to be at the airport to find Timothy.

When I got there, it was warm and the chair was comfortable. But then the police came and moved me on again. They had dogs and they used sign language to tell me I couldn't stay.

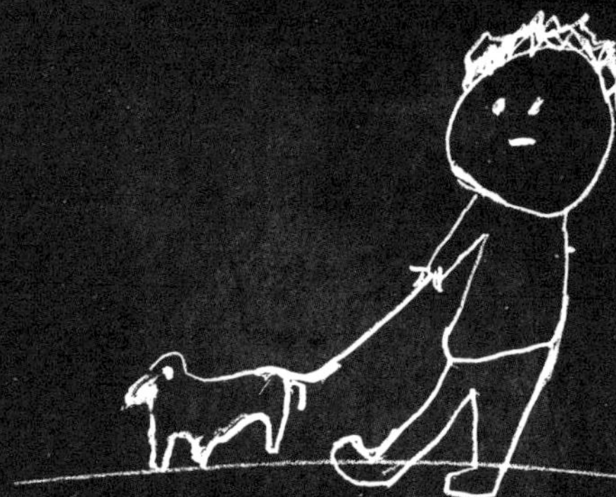

But one lady spoke English. She was Australian. An Australian police lady in Paris! I lifted my hospital gown and showed her my Jilamara t-shirt to show her where I come from. She still hurried me on, but there was a man walking near us.

That man gave me a map of the metro.
'You are Australian,' he said, 'so you need to go to the Australian embassy. It is near the Eiffel Tower.'
He showed me where I needed to get off the train.
He told me to tick off the stations.
'Don't go to sleep,' he said,
'or you will end up in London.'

This time on the metro I was careful to look at the signs. I looked at the map that man had given me, and I ticked them off one by one.

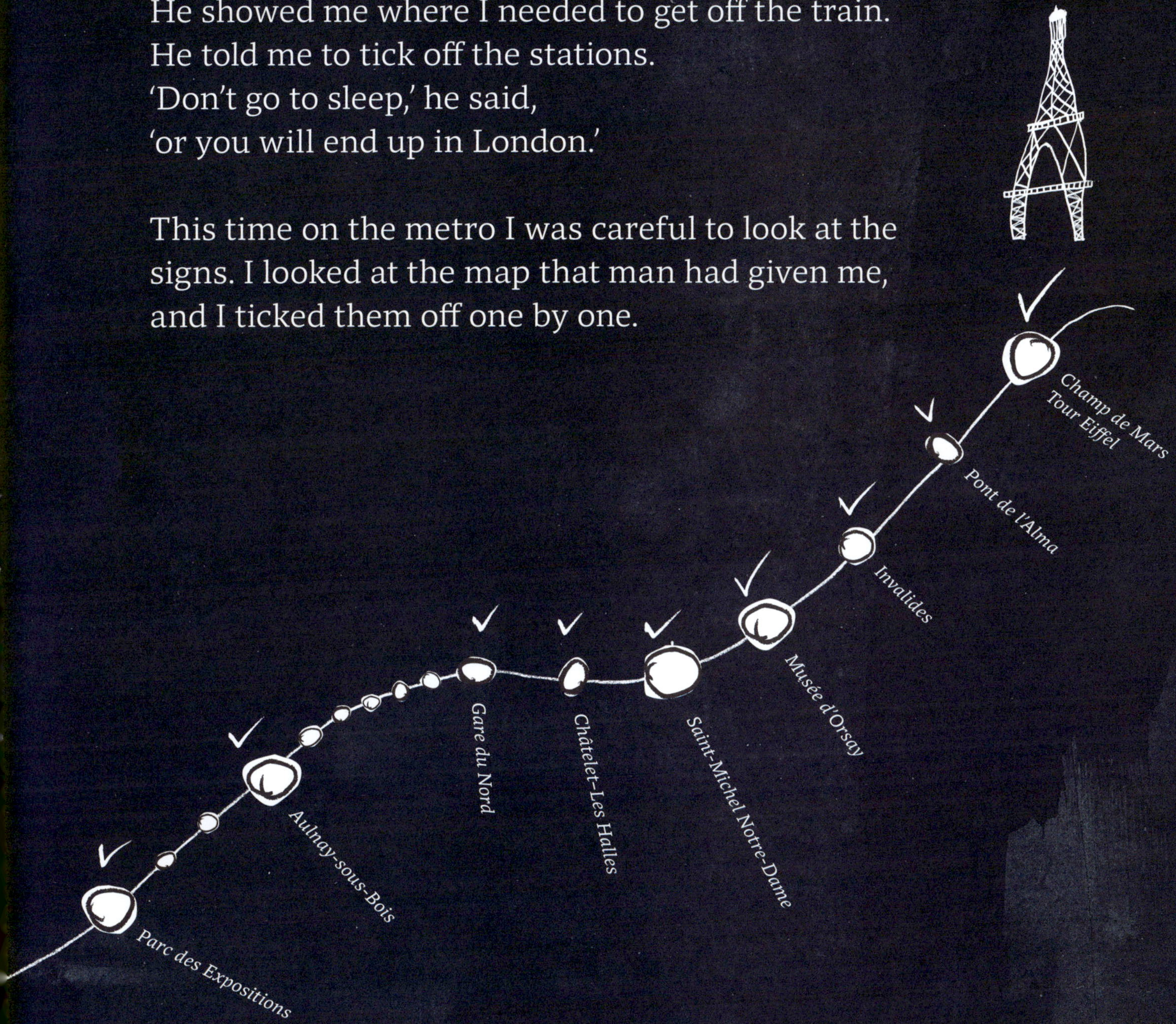

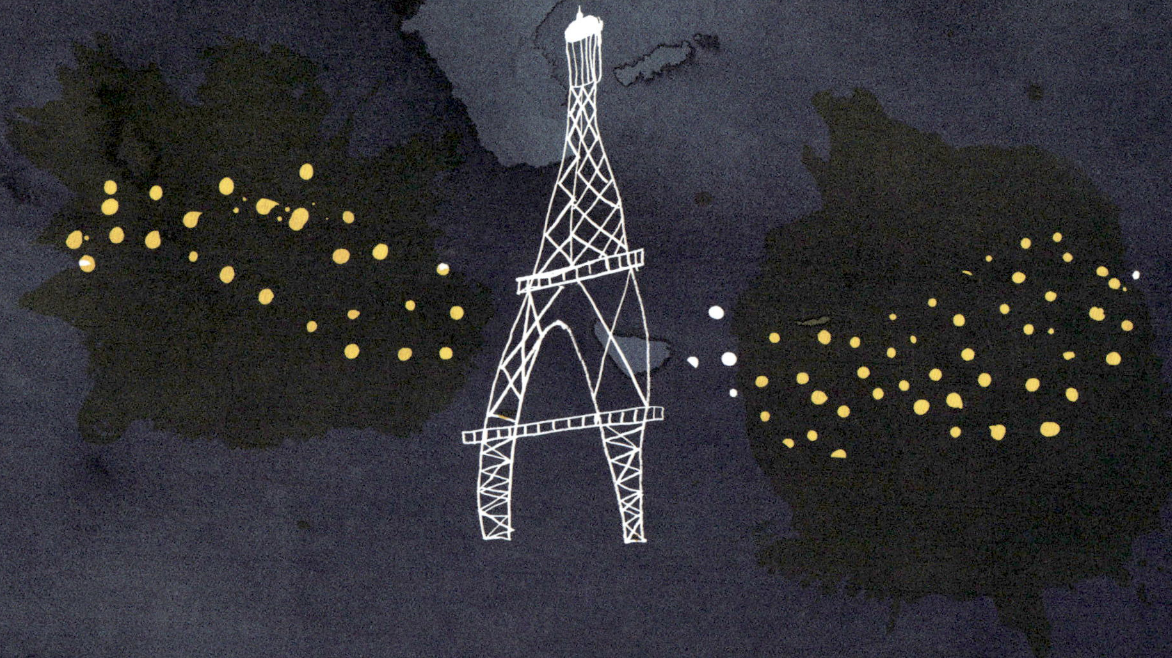

I got off at the Eiffel Tower station.
It was very late at night and the streets were quiet, but there was a guard sitting in his office. He was a Black man too and he gave me a big hug, even though I didn't know him. 'I've seen you on TV!' he said. 'You've been lost in Paris and you're famous!'

He gave me coffee and told me how to find the embassy.

When I got to the embassy I got down on my knees
and I kissed the ground. I saw the emu and the kangaroo
and I knew I was home. I knew it was all alright.
It was early in the morning, maybe 5 or 6 o'clock,
and I sat down to wait.

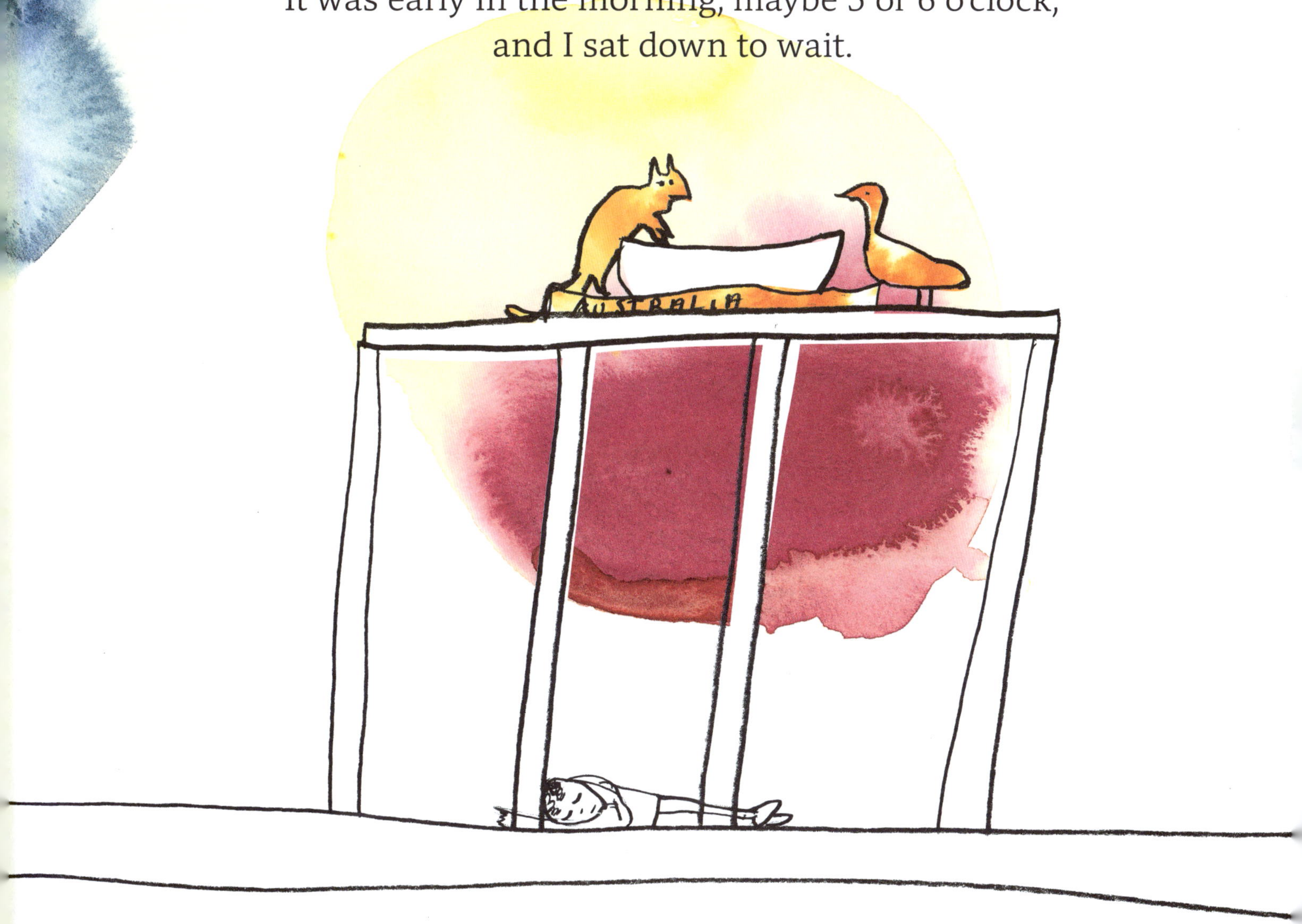

After a while, the door opened and a lady
came out. She was holding her little boy's hand,
bringing him off to school camp.

'Glen Farmer!' she said, 'I know you! My husband
is looking for you. You were reported missing
and now everyone is looking for you!'

Timothy was wild. He shook his head
and spoke to me in Language.
'Ngajiti awani tuwanga!' (Don't do that again!)

'Tell my family I'm okay,' I said.
'Tell Aunty Repi I'm okay.'

Afterwards, the gallery manager took me around
the city on his motorbike.

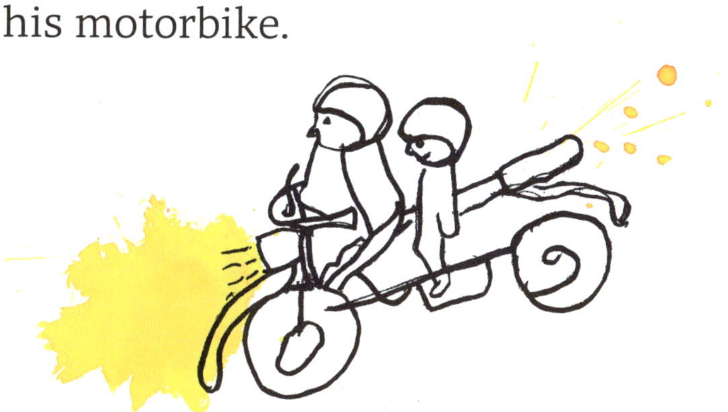

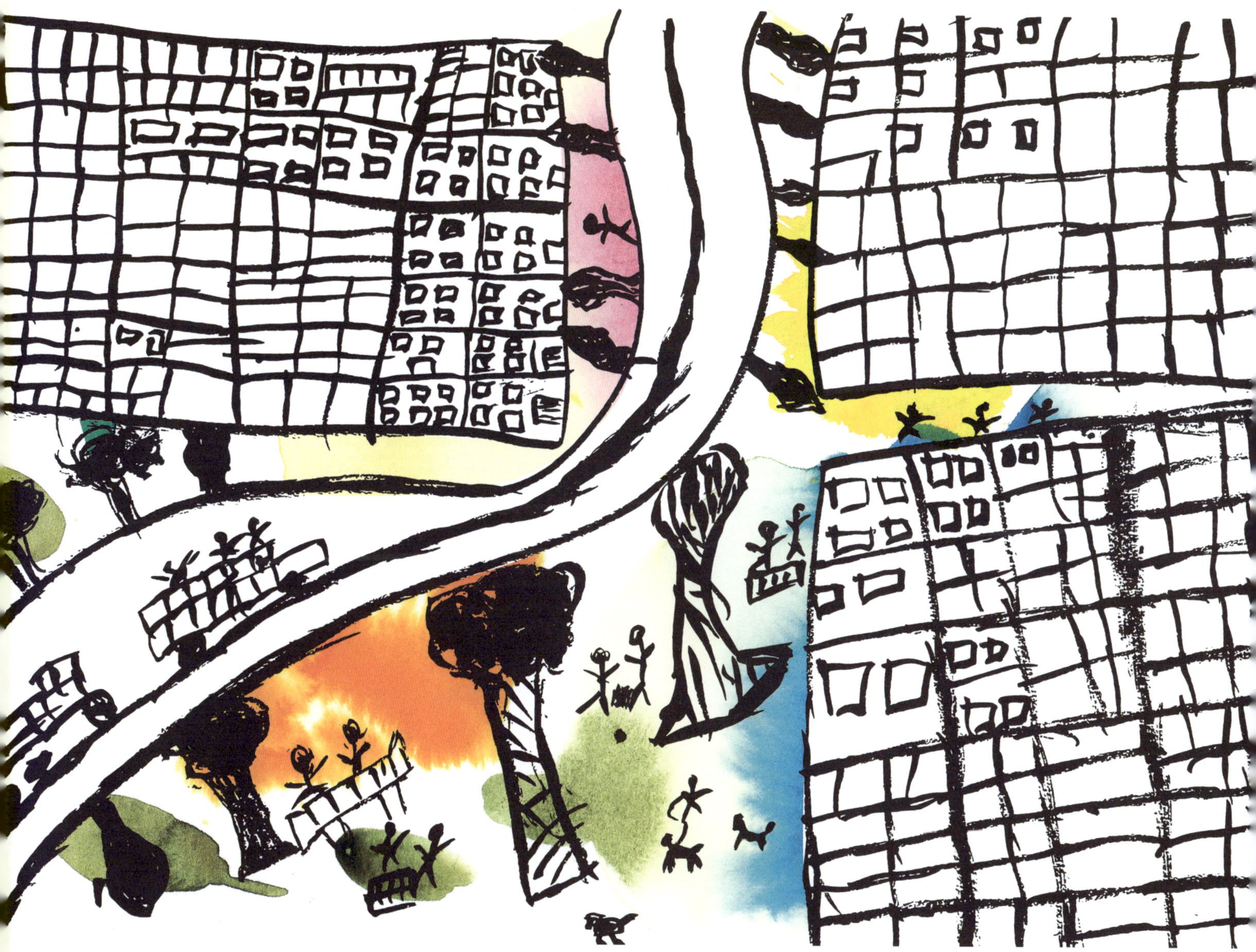

Paris was beautiful.

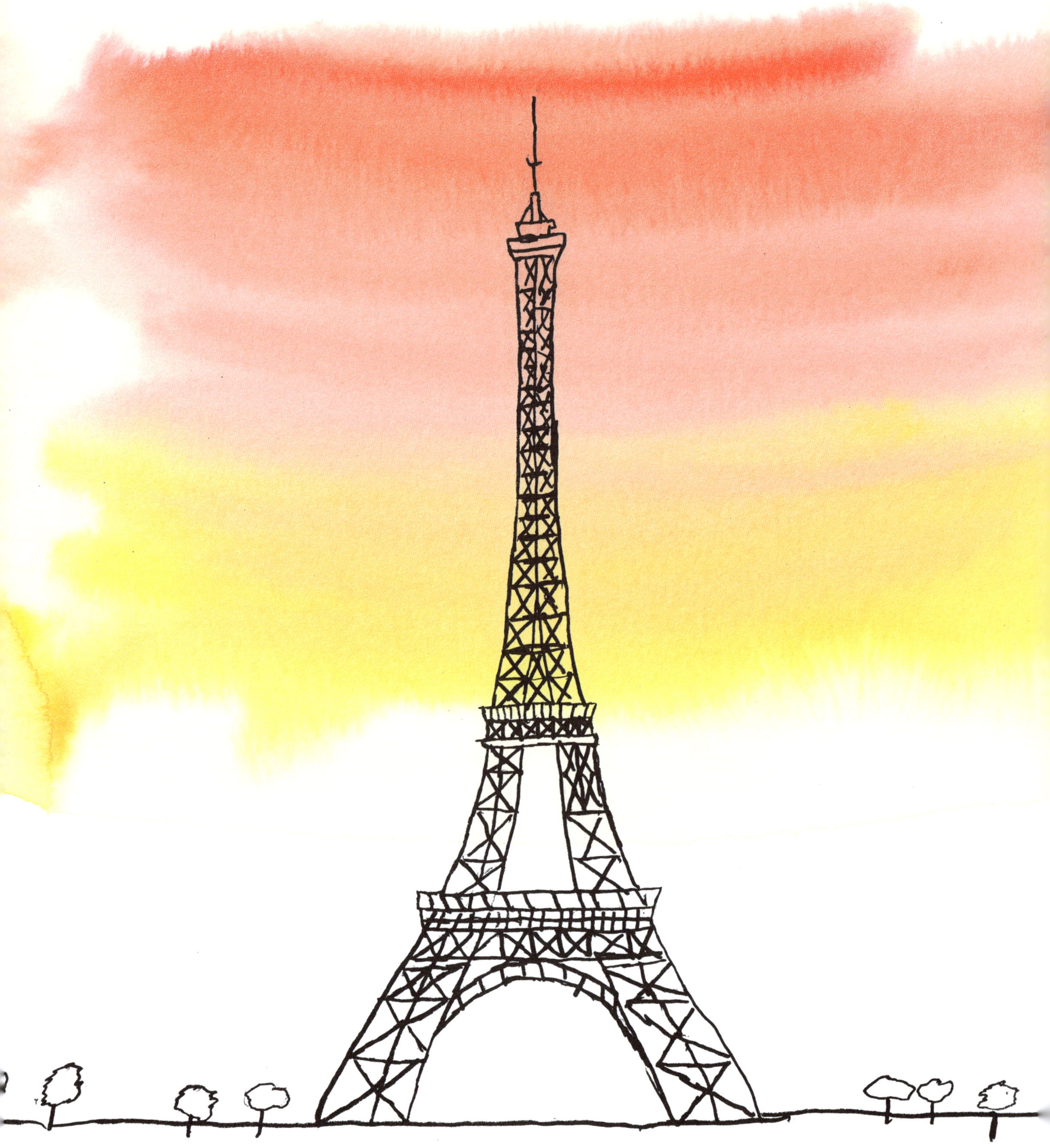

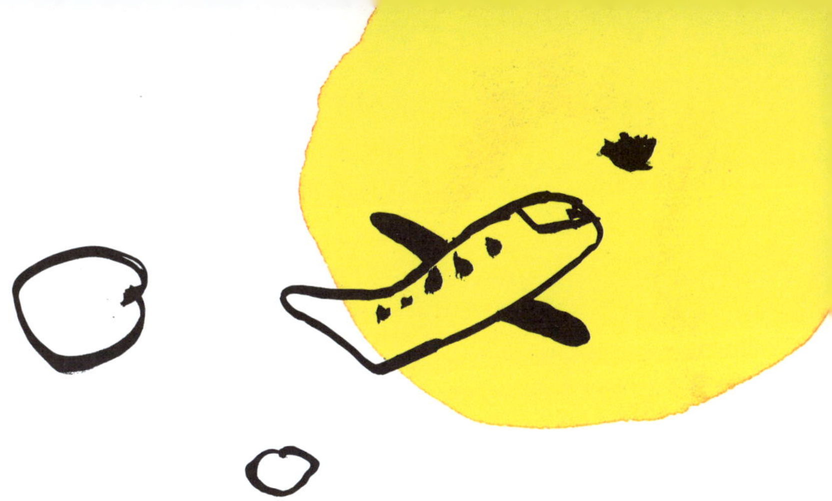

I want to go back one day.

Glen Farmer Illortaminni was born between the mango and mulana trees where the last old house was standing at Milikapiti, Melville Island. He joined Jilamara Arts and Crafts Association in 1994 where he worked for many years as an artist and arts worker. Glen's work has been exhibited across Australia, including in the National Gallery of Victoria and the National Gallery of Australia. Glen also worked at the Muluwurri Museum, a keeping place for Tiwi culture and an important place for remembering the old ways and the Old People.

Today, Glen works for Tiwi Enterprises at Milikapiti farm where he helps grow fruit and vegetables, including pineapples, sweet potato and limes as well as caring for chickens, ducks and friendly water buffaloes. He enjoys travelling, the footy (Go, Tuyu Buffaloes!) and telling stories. Glen likes to go hunting and fishing, and spending time on Country.

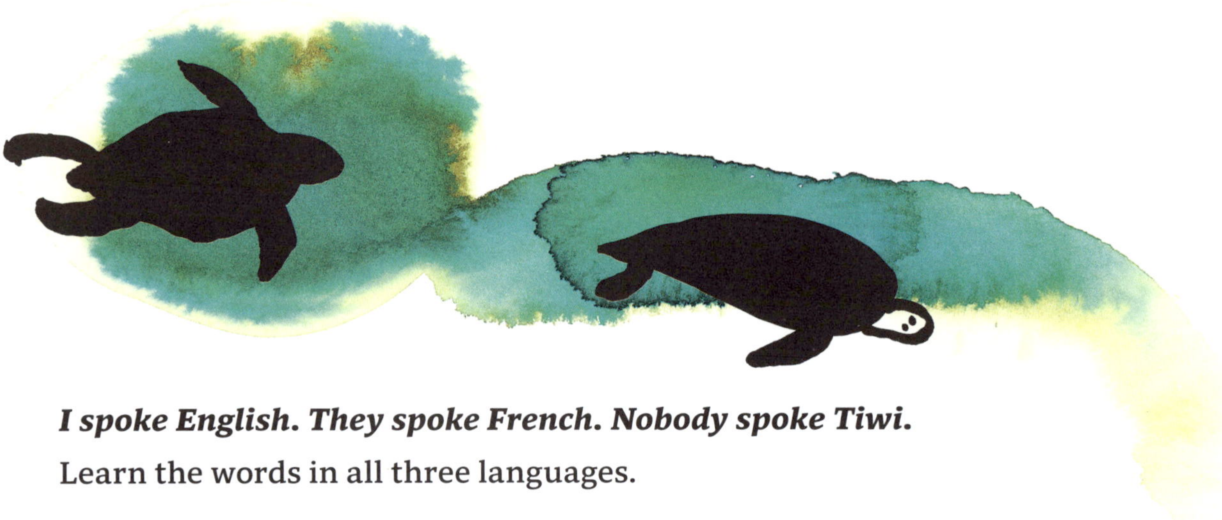

I spoke English. They spoke French. Nobody spoke Tiwi.

Learn the words in all three languages.

Tiwi – English – French

awungana – hello – bonjour

nimpangi – goodbye/see you later – â bientot

nginja awungana yintanga? – what is your name? – comment t'appelles-tu?

kuwa – yes – oui

karluwu – no – non

ngiya kuta-maka – I'm lost – je suis perdu

kuwunawini – money – argent

ningani – today – aujourd'hui

pangarri – tomorrow – demain

nginari – mother – mère

ngirringani – father – père

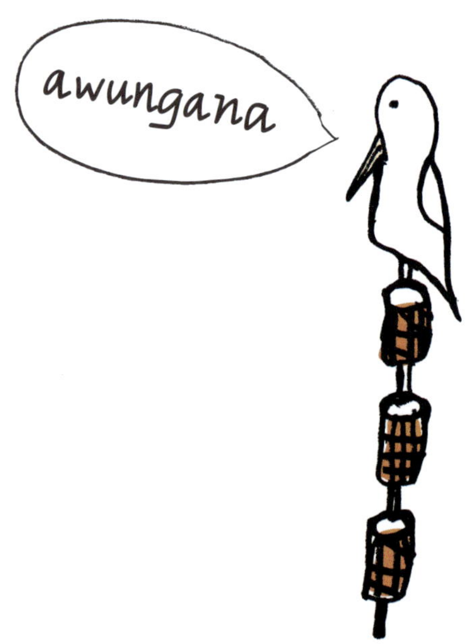

Milikapiti to Paris

distance: 13,710 kilometres

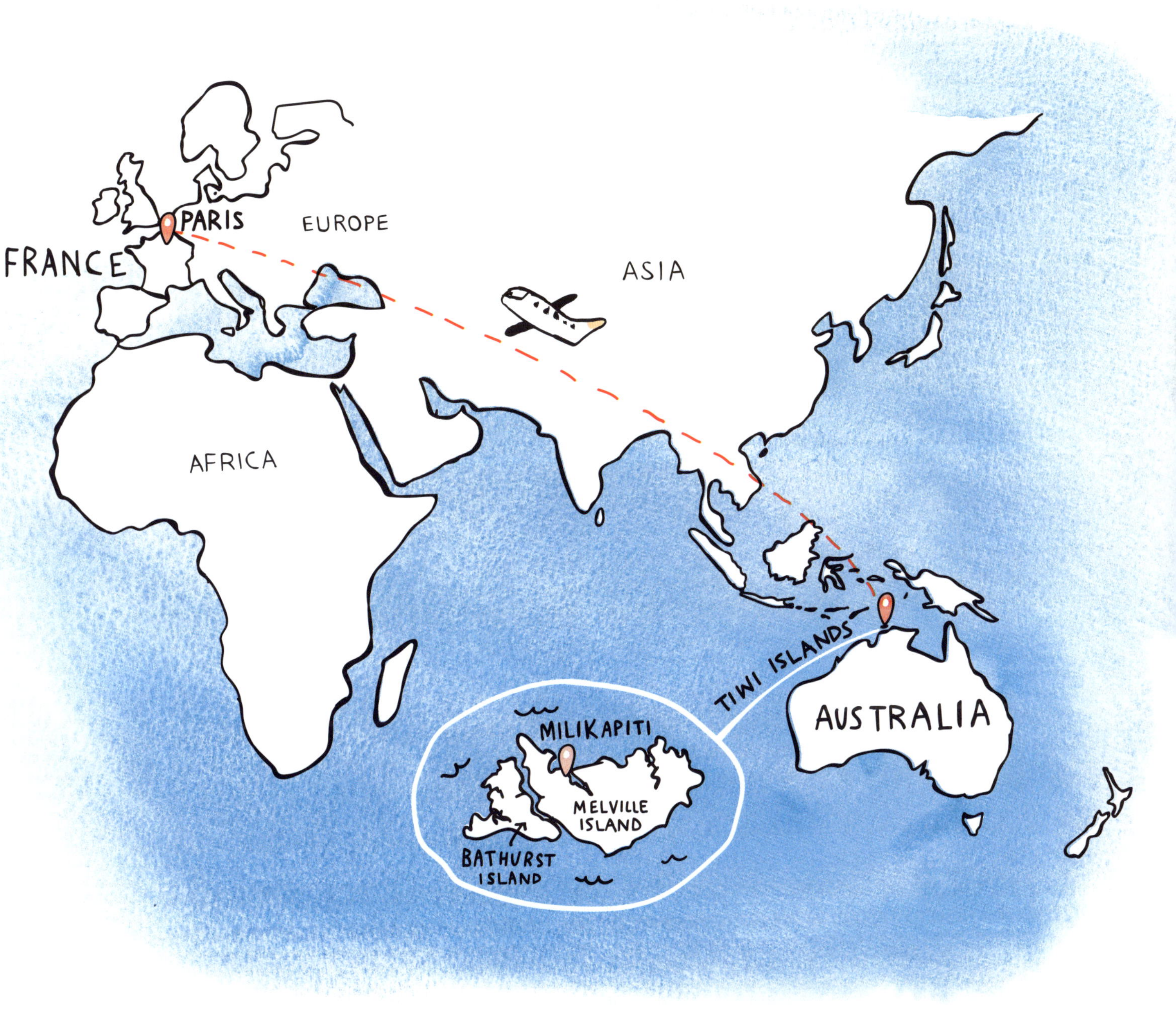

Milikapiti
population: approx. 500

Paris
population: approx. 2.1 million

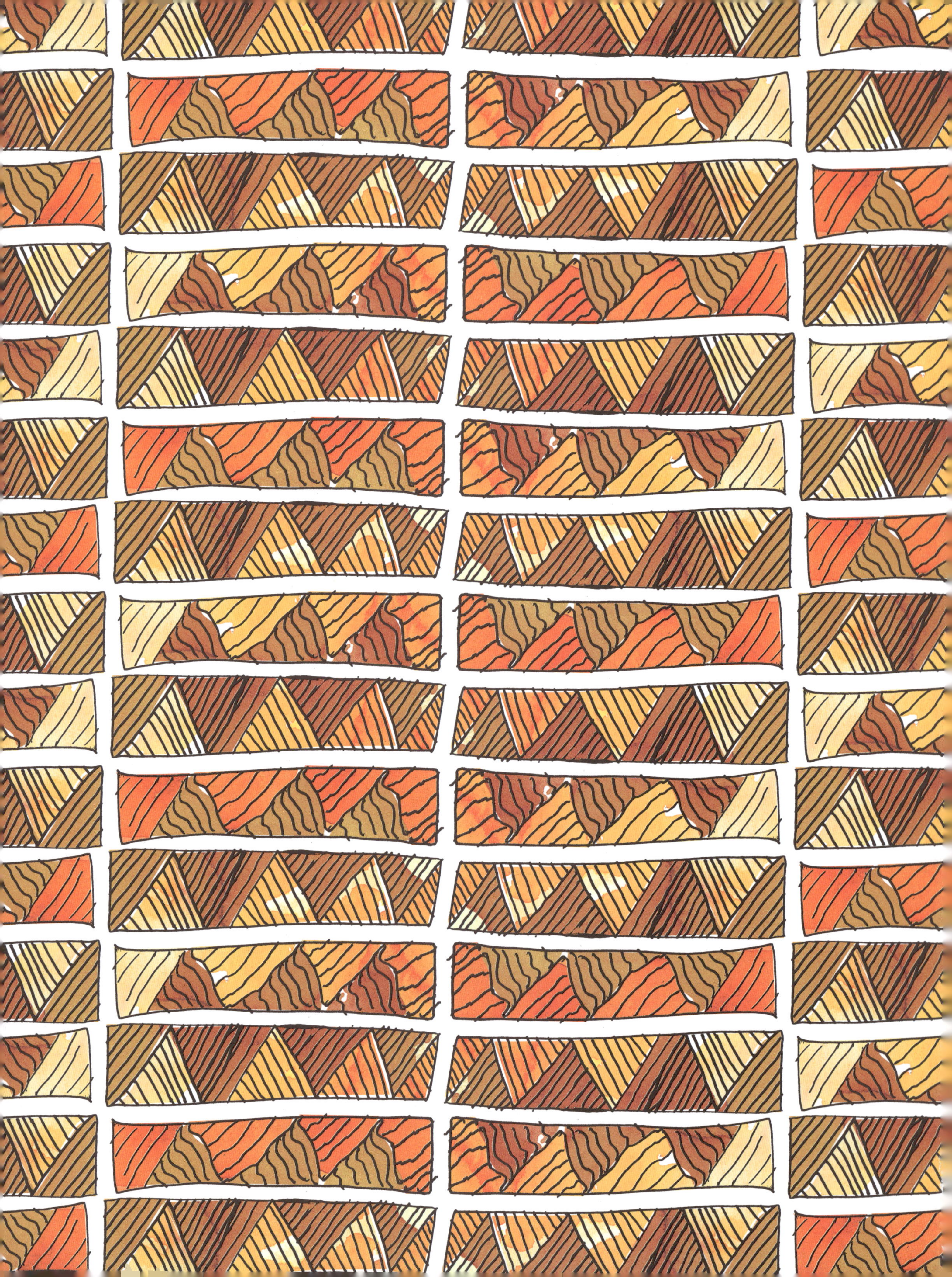